Kissed By My Billionaire Boss

J.P. Sterling

Kissed By My Billionaire Boss

© copyright 2024 J.P. Sterling

Editor: Midnight Owl Editing and Rebecca Carpender

CONTENTS

BLURB

Just one summer in our youth and a memorable first kiss was enough to imprint on my heart forever.

One of the most torturous things a soul can endure is to meet the right person at the wrong time.

For me, it was Graham—a quiet writing recluse with eyes the color of my mother's sapphire ring.

I was the cliché—just a girl next door, a little too naïve to understand life beyond my parents' walls.

Not to mention the queen of wardrobe malfunctions.

Through Graham, life taught me it was often unfair and I was the one who ended up with a broken heart.

I tried to move on, but I never forgot my boy with sapphire eyes.

Then, one day, he stumbled back into my life.

Only this time, he was the guy who signed my paycheck.

Find out what happened when the boy who stole my heart grew up and unexpectedly became my boss.

Kissed by My Billionaire Boss is a clean and wholesome, second-chance, friends to lovers, sweet romance.

Introduction

Welcome to the Autumn-perfect, Christmas-perfect, and falling-in-love-perfect town of Mapleton, Vermont. If this is your first trip to town, sit back and prepare for fun banter and shenanigans to bring you all the feels. If you are returning to Mapleton, welcome home.

Welcome to Mapleton, Vermont

To that summer my friend and I discovered a man named Hemingway. We were thirteen, and we walked to the library—a library that really wasn't in walking distance—way too many times. We read *all* the words on real paper pages which smelled like every grandma's attic, and we were both too young to understand what the words meant.
But boy did we learn.

One

ELINORA

Ten years ago . . .

"Excuse me, do you mind crying a little more quietly?" A raspy voice floated from above my head. I cringed in embarrassment. Someone found me, unsuccessfully hiding behind the only old and knotted tree at the park across from my house. Clenching my eyes, I willed the tears to go away. It was the last day of sophomore year of high school, and I was desperately trying to forget how it had morphed into a horrible day.

Riley had broken up with me. Honestly, I wasn't even that sad about our breakup. I was more upset because Riley was popular—and I had not been before we started dating. Before Riley, I had been repeatedly bullied by the mean girls in school and spent my lunch hours hiding in bathroom stalls. Call it a collision of the stars, but somehow Riley had gotten matched up with me at the tutoring center after he'd failed literature, and—a giant flashing streak of lightning shock—he started to like *me.*

Or maybe he'd only wanted my anatomy lab answers?

Either way, when I'd showed up on his arm at the homecoming game, I'd gained instant respect. I hadn't gotten shoved into one locker while we were dating. Until today when I'd gotten a one-way departure ticket from the cool table to first-class toilet swirlies again. I was pretty sure I was going to corpse-out against this tree. I was being theatrical but I always excelled at language arts.

It was smoldering outside, even for Florida. My tears were mixing with my forehead sweat. I swiped at my eyes until I could clearly see who was speaking to me, and my jaw dropped. He was beautiful, with dramatic, dark cobalt eyes, the same color as the sapphires on my mom's ring, and I immediately froze, forgetting what he had asked of me. "Excuse me but what did you say?"

"I was wondering if you could be quiet."

"Ah, can't you find somewhere else to sit?" I exclaimed, throwing my hands up in exasperation. I wasn't going to back down so easily and squared my shoulders.

He held his neutral expression, clearly not understanding how upset I was. "It's the only shady spot, and my tightwad grandma refuses to turn the air on in my house until June."

"I guess." I muttered as I clumsily slid over, trying to put distance between us while remaining in the shade as much as I could. I wasn't giving in to this rude boy, I just didn't have it in me to fight.

Mumbling indecipherable words under his breath, he plopped down. He was dressed in fashionably ripped jeans and a long-sleeved fleece shirt—something you never see in Florida in May— making it obvious he wasn't from here. He dropped a heavy sigh as he opened the flap on his backpack and retrieved a book with a plain fabric cover.

I was a huge nerd and read *all* the books. Books were life. My interest was full-throttle, and my gaze wandered to the words on the page. It wasn't anything I recognized, and eventually, I let my curiosity win. "What are you reading?"

"*A Movable Feast*." His words came out in one giant, impatient slur without pauses between them.

"Is it a cookbook?" Not having eaten lunch, I inched closer. I was starving since I'd had to return to my third-stall-throne to avoid getting bullied.

"It's Hemingway."

My gut lowered. *Was this guy for real?* I'd read Ernest before as part of my literature class, and he was intense. A deep thinker who strung words together in a way that made me think love was painful yet beautiful to a fault. Most of the boys in the class had yawned through the paragraphs while the girls had gotten all swoony. He must be doing homework. "How is it?"

"Hey, Chatterbox." His gaze flicked up in one quick motion. "If you don't mind, I prefer not to talk."

"Sorry?" It came out more like a question than an apology even though he was the one who'd invaded my space. I lowered my chin, pretending to ignore him while doing my best to sneak a closer look at what he was reading.

"Are you reading over my shoulder?" he asked without looking at me.

"Hmm, more like over your arm," I mused, while noting the specifics of our sitting arrangement. The *sitting arrangement* he'd forced me into and therefore shouldn't complain about.

A sigh hissed from his lips while he dramatically opened the top flap of his book bag, shoved his book back inside, and sprang to his feet.

An undiagnosed urgency budded in my chest, and I jumped up. "What's going on?"

"I just . . .whatever." He had this way of staring at me while seeming to ignore me at the same time.

"Okay, then. Nice chat." I nodded him away.

"That's what I thought." His eyes raked over me before heading back across the street.

I was alone again. *Good.* That was what I had wanted.

I blew out a hard breath when something caught my eye. A notebook was lying in the dirt next to where the new boy had been sitting. I quickly reasoned it must have fallen out of his backpack when he had abruptly stormed off. I scooped it up and was about to call after him, when his silhouette disappeared into Bertha's house. My ancient neighbor, who lived alone and never had company. She wasn't exactly neighborly, and I had zero interest in running into her today.

My eyes returned to the notebook.

Maybe it wasn't important?

Maybe it had something to do with that Hemingway book?

That made me even more curious. Nonchalantly whistling, I pretended to accidentally open the back cover. It was a blank page. I fanned through the pages, but nothing popped out. I was about to consider it unimportant when a few pages in the middle caught my attention.

A beauty delicate like the dewfall and hidden at first.

Awakens my heart, unveiling the worst.

I snuck a glance back at the house, hoping he didn't see me reading his book. With no sign of him, I had to see more.

Gone are the walks on the beach at night.

Gone is the laughter under the moon's white light.

Your smile disappears from my sight,

Taking with it all my delight.

Our journey together must end,

But our memories will forever ascend.

My breath locked in my chest, and my eyes fled back to the beginning. I reread it, letting the words linger on my tongue, feeling every word deep in the pockets of my soul. This guy had barely been able to talk, but boy, did he know how to write. His words were beautiful, and intelligent—everything I would have never guessed him to be. I fanned through the rest of the book and noted dozens of poems and even a few short stories.

My heart wrenched at the imagery that flashed in my mind. With his notebook cradled in my arms, I tossed one final look at the house and with no one in sight, I walked home wondering, who was this guy?

Two

ELINORA

The following morning, I sat at my parents' table, chomping on cold cereal and chugging my morning Cherry coke—drink of champions—when a knock sounded on the door. I wasn't expecting company, and I continued to munch, fully looking like a spicy disaster. My mom called from the foyer, "Elinora, you have a visitor."

With the sassy attitude of a teenage girl, I licked the last soggy remnants of my breakfast from the bowl and dragged my feet to the front door.

The new boy stood next to my dad's baby moose.

As if someone forgot to tell him Florida never gets cold, he wore another fleece shirt and long denim jeans. Was he hiding something under those long sleeves? His dark hair ruffled down past his ears, framing his face in a wild curtain of tousled strands.

"This is our neighbor, Bertha's grandson." Mom gestured to him. "He's from Oregon, but he is here for the summer, helping to take care of her. I mentioned to Bertha last night that you two might enjoy meeting each other. I told her to send him over."

I flicked my hand in a wave while I cowered by the wall. My mom continued to chatter, unaware that we had already met. "I'm sorry, but what did you say your name was?" She leaned closer to him even though she had perfect hearing.

"Graham." He shook his hair out of his face with a flick of his head, revealing his piercing blue eyes while he held his hands politely clasped behind his back and stared forward as if he were in a police lineup.

Watching my mom facilitate this weird setup was a total cringe, as if we were two-year-olds on a forced playdate. "It's nice to meet you, Graham. Please come in. My name is Sharron, and this is Elinora." Mom sidestepped, clearing the space between Graham and me. "I'll let you two get to know each other." She wandered out of the foyer as if she wasn't quite sure where she was going.

Graham wasn't the first boy to come to our house. Riley had stopped over before, but I could tell the whole boy thing made Mom uneasy, because she would never leave me alone with one. She'd find random excuses to loiter nearby, dusting a lamp we never used or pretending to be distracted, while looking out a nearby window. I couldn't blame her, though, because although it was awkward to have her hover, I'd never wanted to be alone with Riley. It wasn't that I hadn't liked him...I did. However, even at sixteen, I wasn't so sure about the rest of the dating stuff I heard gossip about at school.

Graham's eyes slid to the moose that nearly towered over him in the grand foyer. He seemed to be trying to be polite by not asking about it, so I willingly filled him in. "That's Moses. He's a moose."

"I see that." His eyes twinkled at Moses as they bounced from the top to the bottom. "Can I ask why he's in your house?"

"My dad does taxidermy." I reached out to Moses, stroking his fur. "He was too big to put anywhere else, so he lives here."

His expression was steeped in bewilderment. It was cute the way he scrunched his nose like that. Then he showed me his sapphires again. "Are you going to the park today?"

Caught off guard, I played defense. "I didn't realize you could talk so much."

"I still don't know if you can be quiet." His lips were straight, but I caught a glimmer in his eye. The bad attitude he'd been projecting wasn't so much an attitude, it was his odd humor—like a dark horse, he preferred to be somber.

Beautifully somber.

I crossed my arms over my chest. "That's a joke, right?" He didn't reply. My curiosity was piqued when I said, "I can go now if you want."

"Sure." He lowered his lashes, dark and upturned, and I marveled at how there was yet another perfect thing about his eyes.

"Let me grab my sandals." I crossed the foyer and slipped my feet into my favorite pair of in style-ugly flip-flops. Then I grabbed my backpack—knowing I was hiding his notebook in there but feeling so torn because I wasn't ready to give it back—and opened the door. "So, what's wrong with your grandma?"

"She's at the age where she shouldn't be living alone, but she is too stubborn to go into assisted living." He paused while I shut the door, waiting until it latched before he added, "That's the official answer. Honestly, the truth is I got into trouble, so it was the perfect solution to ship me off for the summer." He gazed forward, unfocused as if the sun was glaring too brightly.

We headed down the sidewalk to the park, and I perked an eyebrow in his direction. "What kind of trouble?"

He shrugged indifferently, not expanding despite a slight pulling on the tip of his lips. When he finally latched his eyes up to mine, they seemed to penetrate my soul, sucking out all my secrets. I couldn't be quiet anymore. I hung back as my words floated out softly, "I found your notebook when you were here before. I tried to give it to you, but you had already left."

He stared at me like I had spoken a foreign language. "What did you say?"

I let my backpack slide down my shoulder. Then I unzipped it, taking out the notebook I had stored in there. "Here." I handed it to him. "I'm sorry, not sorry. I read it. Every page."

His eyes flickered to his notebook. "Uh, nobody has ever read my book before."

I bit down on my bottom lip, feeling a tad*ish* guilty. Apparently, I shouldn't have read it, but it was too late now. "Your words are beautiful."

"Thanks." His lashes dipped again. Maybe it was his way of being humble, but I liked him so much more for not being arrogant like the boys at my school.

"Where'd you learn to write like that?" I paced forward gradually, waiting for him to catch up.

"I don't know." He winced as if he was in pain but spoke through it. "I don't like going home. When school is out, I usually go to the library to read or write or whatever." He had this crazy way of staring off as if he was disassociating right in the middle of the conversation.

"Huh." My word wasn't a question as much as a sign that I had heard him. We had reached the park, and I plopped down in front of the oak tree. I did what I always do when it's quiet and looked for something to fidget with. I scanned the grass and settled on plucking a nearby seeded dandelion. As I spun it, the seeds scattered like a million butterflies taking flight. Closing my eyes, I inhaled the delicate scent.

When I opened my eyes again, Graham had taken a step closer, lowering his gaze. "What are you doing?"

"Oh, sorry." I nervously plucked another flower. This one had the perfect golden top, and I tied the stem into a knot and grabbed another dandelion to loop through it to create a chain. I continued to twist the weed into another knot and added another flower to that one. "It's sort of a nervous habit. If I don't know what to say, I fidget. These dandelions make the best chains. It's calming when my anxiety is out of control, and I'm trying not to talk too much."

"So, that's how I can get you to be quiet?" He dropped down, sitting next to me. "All I have to do is find you some weeds." I took delight in the sound of his snicker.

"Some see weeds." My lips pulled into a thoughtful smile. "I see a wish."

A door slammed across the street, and his grandma wobbled to the front of the porch, leaning on her walker. In her gruff smoker's voice, she hollered over the porch rail, "Time to eat."

"Be right there!" He obediently stood and brushed off his pants.

I caught sight of his notebook, and quickly picked it up, reaching it out toward him. "Here."

He shot me a casual sideways glance. "Nah, it's your turn."

My brow furrowed together. "For what?"

A daring glint sparkled out of the deepest cobalt of his eyes. "Write something."

"Um, I'm not a writer."

"You can find something you want to talk about." He tilted his head a slight measure closer to me. "I know you know how to talk." He pointed to the book, tacking on, "There's a pen in the spine."

Flashing a coy smile, I hugged the book closer to my chest. "Are you trying to find another way to get me to shut up?"

"Totally." Then, true to his introverted fashion, Graham pushed his hands in his pockets, offered me a quiet smile, and sulked across the street. I was left sitting by the tree with his notebook and a perfectly weighted fountain pen. But even with my fancy pen, I had a bigger issue. Writing had never been my thing. I was a prolific reader, but I would get itchy when I had to write. If there was ever a word to define how a brain could become instantly uncoordinated by the touch of a pen, that would be my main adjective, but I didn't want to let him down. I tried.

Roses are red

Violets are…something that rhymes with sapphires?

Flat tire?

Bonfire?

This was bad. I scribbled again but then quickly scratched that out too. I decided I wasn't great with the whole tortured love poetic thing he had going on, and I went in a new direction. I left the book propped against the tree and went home with this on the top page:

Roses of night
Violets on the ground
I don't like to write
'cause words need sound.

That day started our slow friendship. He never had too much to say. It didn't stop him from coming over and asking me to hang out every day. We'd mostly waste time. I chatted, stringing wishes together until we finally used the last one that spring brought. The best thing we did was pass that notebook back and forth. He always had something new he'd written, and I always had something sassy to comment back.

Things were routine until midsummer. The day started with a shopping trip with my friend, Bre. She was my only school friend, and I hadn't seen her all summer. Even though we enjoyed each other's company, our friendship had always been one of convenience in that we only had each other at school. I was one of those curvy girls who developed way too soon but then never stopped. Bre was small, like the runt of the runtiest litter. Our size discrepancy made all the mean kids refer to us as Pooh and Piglet. I don't think I looked even close to Pooh, but Bre had these pale blue eyes. Plus, she appeared so timid all the time. I couldn't help but think she resembled Piglet, and I was protective of her. I did my best to stick up for her, but most of the time that resulted in me being bullied. It was a lose-lose situation we tolerated—together.

"So, are you looking for anything special?" Bre asked before wrapping her lips around her straw and loudly slurping the remnants of her blueberry-lime Italian soda while we passed the decorated windows of the trendy boutiques on Main Street.

"Yeah," I said thoughtfully. I had a budget that required me to use almost all the babysitting money I had saved. "I need some makeup and a new shirt. If I can find a pair of pants that doesn't make me look like I'm stuffed sausage, that would be great, too."

"Ugh." Bre stuck her bottom lip way out and blew a stream of her breath up, making the tips of her bangs waver. For the record, I had told her not to cut bangs in the summer. I knew they'd stick to her forehead, but she hadn't listened. "It's too hot to wear makeup this time of year. Don't you think so?"

"I want to try something new." I smiled coyly. "Maybe try to look a little older."

Shooting me a suspicious glance, she asked, "Are you trying to win Riley back?"

Almost shuddering at the mere suggestion, I firmly stated, "No." Then I motioned to the salon on the corner. "I think they have makeup samples right in the front of the store." Taking my lead, she followed me through the glass door. The air was now densely permeated with perfumed scents that tickled my nose. I scanned the displays along the counter, reading all the names of fruity lip-gloss. That's exactly the thing I would have normally shopped for, but today I strolled past this counter to the section of full coverage lipsticks. I carefully selected a peachy-nude matte color like the ones I always saw in fashion magazines paired with smokey eyes.

Bre didn't join me in shopping for makeup, but instead loitered by the checkout stand, flipping through a magazine. "Look, you should read this one." She held up one cover, flashing the headline at me. "The Top Ten Rules of how to be a Great Kisser." She flipped it open, fanning through the pages until she found the advertised article. I didn't reply, but she continued to read, "Number one, check that your breath is not offensive."

I snickered, not because I had any experience with kissing, but that seemed like a no-brainer.

"Number two," she read on, "once you have their attention, lean closer. Number three: close your eyes. Number four—"

I interrupted her, "Let me guess." I paused, considering what would be the next most obvious thing. "Don't burp in their mouth."

She giggled, sticking her tongue out in disgust. "No, it says to make sure you tilt your head so you don't bump into each other's noses."

"Psh, seriously?" I reached out, ripped the magazine from her hands, and replaced it on the stand. "That article is dumb. Who doesn't know all that?"

"Ah, a girl who has never been kissed." Her eyes were wide, possibly embarrassed. Which is the precise reason I'd taken the article away from her. I didn't want to hear about all the things I didn't want to know about. And besides, I had my makeup and was ready to leave.

When I walked through the door that night, my mom greeted me with her good apron on—the one with pink lilies. She usually reserved it for Easter or other important dinners. "Bertha had an accident." Her voice was hushed. "She's in the hospital. Everything's mostly fine, but she has to wait for a hip replacement. Graham was up there all day, but I invited him over for dinner. The poor boy hasn't eaten a meal all day."

Her words sent a lightning bolt right through my ears to my gut that ricocheted back up, making my eyes round out. "Graham is coming here. Tonight?"

"Yeah." Her eyes paced my face as if searching for clues, and she pinched her lips together. "It seems like you two are getting along. You're meeting at the park every day."

I hated it when my mom pinched her lips. Pinching told me she meant something way different than what was actually said. I could tell she was assuming, but she wasn't one to ever come out and ask. We never had that kind of chatty mother-daughter relationship. To throw off her assumptions,

I tossed an annoyed shoulder in her direction, trying to appear like I couldn't care less. "He's fine."

Perfectly on cue, a rapid knock sounded on the front door, and my mom spun on her heel and called, "Come in." The door slowly opened. Graham appeared, hovering on the threshold, unsure of what to do next. Mom made a grandiose gesture waving him farther into the house. "You're just in time."

He carefully closed the door behind him. "Thank you so much for the invitation," he said without a hint of a smile.

"It's my pleasure." Mom went on in her gracious hostess voice as she continued to lead Graham to the formal dining room—the room we only used on holidays. My dad sat stiffly at the table as if he was a forlorn passenger in an airplane which had been sitting on the tarmac for days with no evidence of ever being able to take flight.

When I said we never used this room for anything other than holiday dinners, I left out one part. The part about how my dad had adopted this room as a showcase for his taxidermy creatures. Snakes and rodents lined the walls, and each corner bore a larger animal, the coyote and full-sized bear being his most prized specimens. I was used to them and hardly noticed, but it was quite hilarious to see Graham's eyes latch on to the grizzly bear as he took a seat across from me.

"Your animals are...interesting," Graham complimented my dad. Directly above him loomed a giant mountain lion head, frozen with his jaw lurching forward, teeth snarling out.

"Thanks." Dad's eyes flashed up to his prized mountain lion. "I feel safer with them around."

Graham slumped down into his chair, keeping a straight face. "Is there a reason all the ferocious ones are glaring at me?"

My dad threw his head back in laughter, obviously amused. Instead of carrying on with the joke, he abruptly halted his chuckle, then deadpanned on Graham. "Animals have a sixth sense for things."

"Stop," Mom elbowed Dad as she came up behind him, holding the lasagna pan with two of her best potholders. Now I knew something was up because her potholders always had burnt holes in them. These potholders looked brand new. She leaned over, placing the dish in the center of the table. In an apologetic tone, she spoke to Graham, "He's teasing."

My gaze bounced from Mom to Dad, and then over to Graham. I was desperate for clues as to why my dad was acting like this. I grabbed the salad bowl, helped myself to a plateful, and passed it to my mom. Nobody said anything. The only sound was the crunch of carrots smashing between my dad's molars. Over and over. I didn't think he would ever stop chewing.

He was a juicer, alienating every pulp.

Thankfully, the salad course didn't last for all of eternity, and the lasagna was much more soothing to masticate. Usually, I was the chatty one who would keep the conversation going through dinner, but I was frozen. My dad shoved food into his mouth without looking at it because his eyes were squared on Graham. Graham hardly touched his food as his large pupils seemed to waiver between the lion, the grizzly, and Dad.

The kissing article Bre and I had read popped into my head. Talk about bad timing. For no sane reason I can fathom, I found myself staring at Graham's lips. Heat burned my cheeks when I imagined pressing my lips into his, and I quickly turned my gaze down to my plate.

When dinner was finally over, my mom collected the plates and spoke to Graham in a thoughtful voice, "I suppose you'll have to stay at the house alone tonight. I'll check in on Bertha at the hospital, but if either of you need anything, let me know."

I waited for his response, expecting him to comment about his mom or dad, or someone else who'd be around. Instead of declining my mom's offer, he simply said, "Thank you." Then as quietly as he had been the last hour, he left.

I stared out the front picture window, watching him walk down the walkway. When I finally turned back to my mom, she was nervously pacing behind me. Something she never does. *What is really going on?*

Three

GRAHAM

It was way too early for normal people when the tap came on the door. Pulling my eyes open, I quickly realized I had fallen asleep on my grandmother's sofa. From the number of pink flowers on the couch, you'd think it would have smelled like potpourri, but the flowers were merely a façade. The cushions had been steeped in Grandma's stale cigarette smoke, choking me with each deep inhalation. Not that breathing was ever easy for me unless I was on the football field. I didn't have asthma or anything medical. If I had to self-diagnose, I'd say it was what happened when one was used to being mistreated.

"Boy, those social workers never take any time off." I moved slowly, not bothering to check the side window before I swung open the door. Instead of seeing my social worker, I was dismayed to see Elinora standing there in her cut-off jean shorts and retro Army T-shirt. As far as I knew, she wasn't in the Army, nor did she know anyone in it, but she looked hot in gray because it contrasted the deep shade of hazel in her eyes.

"Hey." She eagerly greeted me from behind a stack of clear food containers. "My mom said your grandma can't come home today. She put together some meals for you."

I scratched the back of my head, overwhelmed by the kindness. Nobody had ever brought me food before, let alone cared if I ate. "Ah, thanks, I guess." I reached forward, took the stack of containers, and turned on my heel, assuming she'd leave. Okay, by now, I knew her enough to expect she'd have something *else* to say. I let one eye linger on her, waiting. And sure enough, she went right into chatterbox mode.

"Do you have plans for today?"

Wincing through my light-sensitive eyes, I replied, "Ah, it's sort of early to have my day planned."

"Noon isn't that early," she quipped back with full caffeinated energy.

"Is it really that late?" I flashed my gaze across the room to the antique cuckoo clock on the wall, confirming it was in fact noon. I said aloud, but more to myself, "Hmm, I guess so."

"If you don't have any plans, my mom said you can come over. You know, in case you get bored or whatever." She smashed the toe of her flip-flop into the door I was holding, as if trying to butt in a little more. With bright pink toenails and a silver toe ring flashing on the biggest toe, it was too much teenage girl spunk for me. Even though she was cute, I'd learned not to get my hopes up when it came to girls. Or really anyone.

"It's cool," I muttered, stretching my hand over my head, still trying to wake up. "I'm fine here unless you want to hang out?"

"I would, but for some odd reason my mom said I can only see you if you're inside my house with supervision." One of her eyebrows spiked above the other. "I think it's my dad's new rule, and it's absurd, if you ask me."

The thing was, I loved hanging out with her, as it sort of became my lifeline of normality this summer. I couldn't stomach my nerves when I was near her parents. I knew what Ron thought of me. I could see it in his eyes every time he looked at me. I didn't mean any disrespect toward him because he was protecting his daughter, but I also didn't care what he thought of me. I had learned to shut down my feelings. I wasn't going into that house again as long as I could help it. "Ah, I'll have a bite to eat and then see."

"Sure." Her lips spread into one of her flirty smiles, the one that made her eyes twinkly, and she spun on her heel, waving as she walked down the steps. "You know where to find me."

I waved until she'd turned all the way around, and then I shut the door. Now, I was left thinking about her smile. Even though her mouth spent way too much time talking, it was beautiful, like the rest of her.

I carried my food to the kitchen. It couldn't have come at a better time because I was starving. I opened the lid on the first container. Leftover lasagna. Smelling it before deciding to forget a plate, I nuked the whole dish in the microwave. Afterall, it was already noon. I was about to take a bite when a knock sounded on the door again.

I slid my chair back and got up. As I passed in front of the door, my heart sank at the neatly wrapped dark-brown hair bun that flashed in the window. I pushed the screen door open, knowing there was no point in pretending I didn't know why she was there.

"Good morning, Graham." Sylvia wearily smiled as she pushed her way through the door. Sylvia was the newest social worker recently assigned to my "case" since I moved in with Grandma. Fresh out of school, she still held that optimistic I'm-going-to-change-the-world attitude all the newbies have. "How are you?"

I leaned against the wall, as if merely standing took all my energy. "How am I supposed to be?"

"I got a call from the hospital." She had one of those nasally voices that was so distracting, it made me cringe. "The nurse had reason to think your grandma will not be able to come home soon, because she does, in fact, need a hip replacement.

They plan to transition her to a nursing home for six weeks since there is no one here who is over eighteen.”

I held my breath, knowing what was coming.

“I tried to get a hold of your mom, but it seems like her phone has been disconnected.” Her eyes hovered over mine. “Do you have a better number to reach her?”

I shrugged but didn’t offer any sound.

“Okay, then,” she went on in a slower voice. “I’m afraid I’m going to recommend you for temporary foster care until—”

“What?” I jolted, standing up straight. “Why can’t I stay here?”

Her brow furrowed before she said very quietly, “You can’t stay alone because you’re only sixteen, and the state won’t allow it.”

“What foster care?” My chest collapsed, remembering the last time I’d tried that. It hadn’t ended so well.

“I don’t know yet.” She rolled her bottom lip under her top row of teeth before steeling her lips into an obviously forced grin. “I’ll find you something comfortable.” Her gaze flashed outside. “Your grandmother did say the neighbor was checking on you.” She pointed to the house next door. “Is it this house right here?”

“Yeah,” I muttered so low I couldn’t even hear my own words.

Her pity-filled eyes shined back at me. I hated it. “I will run over there to chat with them and let them know the situation. Then, I'm headed back to the office to make some calls. Hopefully, by the end of the day I'll be back to take you to a new home." Her lips pulled into an uncomfortable wince before she corrected herself, "Er, you know. Not a home but a place to stay for now." With the compassion of a hammer, she patted my shoulder as if I were a giant baby with a burp that wouldn't come out. "Everything is going to be fine." Avoiding eye contact, she tucked her head and walked back down the steps. My fingers curled into a fist as she returned to her shiny, new SUV like all was well with the world. It was just another day at work for her.

Destroying lives one life at a time. I squeezed my fist tighter, my nails digging into my skin. There's no way I was going to foster care.

I could run away.

It was a serious thought.

However, I was still on probation, which for sure would put me into juvie. But would juvie be worse than a foster home? It was all so lame. I was not a child. I wrung my hands together, mulling over my options.

I could take care of myself.

I always had.

It was all a stupid game to these people until I became unreachable. I'd go ghost before I'd allow anyone to send me to a lame foster home. As I paced back to the living room, my eyes fell on my notebook, sitting in the middle of Grandma's coffee table. I plopped down on the couch, opened it and scribbled:

Dear whatever doesn't kill me:

It's me and I don't want to have to be stronger. I'm strong enough. Kindly leave me alone.

Four

Elinora

It wasn't overly late, but I had already dressed for bed, wearing cotton pajama pants—the ones with pink clouds. My hair was still wet and wrapped in a messy bun when the doorbell rang. I focused on reading my book—Little Women—in my pillow pile while I waited for someone else to get it. It only took another moment, and I heard muffled voices.

Footfalls echoed in the hall. My mom's voice lightly called, "Elinora."

"Yeah," I replied without putting my book down.

The door opened, Mom's face sliding through the crack, pinching in a way that wasn't common for her, but her eyes were soft. "Are you busy?"

"Just reading."

She pushed the door open, easing another step forward. "Do you want to come back downstairs? We have company."

My spine pulled straight as I dropped my book into my lap. "We do?"

"Graham from next door needs a place to stay." Unsure how it was even possible for her voice to lower even more, I leaned forward to hear her. "He's going to be here just for tonight."

A sarcastic chuckle leaked out of my mouth. "Isn't he old enough not to need a babysitter?"

Her eyes layered with caution as she stole a glance down the stairs. She must have been satisfied with what she saw because she crossed the room and sat next to me on my bed. "I'm not sure how much to say, because it's a sensitive situation, but he's been in some trouble. And his—"

"Right," I quipped, remembering Graham had told me that.

"He's under probation and isn't supposed to stay alone for days like he has been, but his social worker can't find a place for him to stay."

One of my brows hiked when I asked, "What did he do?"

Her lips pulled tight into a straight line, and her eyes gently traced my face. I soaked up the silence, aware of how secretive my mom was being. We had never been the mother-daughter duo who talked about stuff, but I could tell she was holding back.

"Mom, just spit it out. Is he a giant psycho?"

"There are protective measures in place for juveniles, and I agree with them. He doesn't need everyone to know his private life. I would rather not say anything, but no, he isn't crazy. He's had a very tough life, and because of that, he was put in some difficult situations—"

"What are you saying?" She was feeding me a bunch of baloney.

"I'm saying, we will all respect his privacy. He's going through some rough stuff, and he doesn't have anyone to help him. He has a social worker, but she is failing to find placement for him since he can't share a home with other foster children because he has a criminal record—"

"Criminal?" I blurted out. "This doesn't even sound like you. Why would you let him come here?"

"He's Bertha's grandson." She nodded curtly at me, like it hurt for her to answer more questions. "She's worried. She's all he has right now. It's a huge mess because she is temporarily disabled. And, I think we can be nice to him for one night."

I stilled my face into a flat expression. "And by that, you mean don't ask questions but come downstairs and hang out?"

She slid off the bed, lingering her gaze on me until I followed her. I didn't mind hanging out with him. Actually, he was the best friend I'd ever had, but the way my parents were acting made me insanely curious.

Curious and a little afraid.

Mom led the way downstairs into the family room, where I expected my perfect-hostess mom to have spread out board games and other entertainment options, but my dad had different ideas. Dad sat in front of the coffee table with his taxidermy project laid out in front of him on a sheet. My mom's breath caught loudly in her throat. "Ron, do you really think you need to do that now while we have company?" Her eyes drifted to Graham, who sat opposite him on the same sofa.

"He doesn't mind." Dad kept his eyes low on a flattened squirrel he methodically rolled in his hand, reminding me of how those dads on TV shows cleaned a shotgun on the porch when their daughters got picked up for a date. Dad never did his taxidermy on the living room coffee table. This was obviously some sort of warning sign for Graham because he was a boy, and he was in my house. My face heated as I backed against the wall.

"The trick to getting a realistic animal is to hide the incision." My dad was obviously speaking to Graham but kept his eyes low on his squirrel. Graham had his hands stuffed in his sweatshirt pockets, avoiding looking directly at the dead squirrel. My dad continued his creepy tutorial. "I like to start by placing a tiny slit in the throat and slice them all the way through because that is an easy spot to hide an incision."

Cringing so hard, I begged Mom with my look to stop Dad, but she appeared as nervous as I felt. We squinted through narrowed eyes and watched as my dad deliberately—excruci-

atingly slowly—slit the throat of the squirrel and then proceeded to cut down the length of the body. I turned my head,
feeling sick. "Dad, this is disgusting. Can't you take it to the
garage?"

"Well, I could, but I thought it was a nice way for Graham
and me to get to know each other."

I peered at my mom, who was still avoiding the squirrel too.
"If this is about Graham, may I please be excused?"

Her eyes washed over my dad. When he said nothing, my
mom replied, "Why don't you and I go into the kitchen and
make us all a snack?"

"Deal." I was out of the room before my mom could even
stand. When my mom joined me in the kitchen, I harshly
whispered to her, "What is Dad doing?"

She pressed her lips together for a moment. "He's a little
apprehensive about Graham being here...with you."

Feeling defensive that his actions had anything to do with
me, I flattened my palm on my chest. "Me?"

She raised one shoulder as if she was trying to brush any
concern away. I didn't buy it because I could see the jitters in
her fingers. "You know, dads and their daughters."

"This isn't funny, Mom. Dad is acting like a psycho. What
did Graham do?"

My mom opened the cupboard in front of me but immediately shut it without looking inside, revealing again her
anxiety. Then she scooted to the next cupboard—the one

with actual snacks—and pulled out a bag of popcorn and another half-empty bag of pretzels. She emptied both bags into a big bowl and stated in an oddly calm voice, "I wonder if he even got any dinner. Maybe I should make Graham a sandwich?" She pivoted and opened the refrigerator door.

Frustration coursed through my veins, and I balled my hands into fists. This perfectly cloned model of a fifties housewife was casually making a sandwich for our house guest, but she was not my mom. *That psycho in the living room is definitely not my dad.* We were never an overly communicative family, but they also never kept obvious secrets from me. I wanted to scream. I pleaded, "Mom, what did he do?"

"Let's see. Turkey. Cheese." She inventoried the ingredients as she grabbed them.

"Mom!"

"Elinora." Her tone was easy, irking me so full of annoyance that pressure expanded in my head.

"What did he do?" I pressed with aggression in my tone because at this point, she owed me an answer. She had allowed me to be his friend all summer, never hinting a word about this. Suddenly, when he had to stay the night in my house, my parents were acting out of their minds.

She shoved the fridge door with her hip, then spread the ingredients on the counter. "I would tell you, because I actually don't see it fully as his fault, but your father isn't comfortable with, well, any of this."

"Then why did you ask me to come downstairs?" I said through my clenched teeth. "I didn't even know he was here. I could have stayed in my room."

"I had no idea your dad would act like this." She assembled his sandwich and set it on the table, then signaled a little too intensely with her head to the bowl.

I carried the bowl with straight arms as if it weighed fifty pounds while my mom murmured, "Go tell Graham to come back here. We need to get him away from your dad. I think your father will be in there for a while."

I kept my not-happy glare but obediently dragged my feet back down the hall to find my dad still in narrator mode. "This is some of the strongest string you can find. I wrap it around the packing, so it keeps its shape." He held the wire like he was about to create a noose. Graham's eyes were wide when they landed back on me, pleading for rescue.

Clearing my throat, I announced, "My mom made you a sandwich, but you have to eat it in the kitchen."

I'd never seen a human fly across a room as fast as Graham. I doubted he was even hungry—especially after watching what my dad just did—but relief washed over his face when he escaped. He bellied up to the table, and I plopped down on a chair across from him. I assumed my mom would hover over us, but she headed back to the living room with my dad. Muffled voices wafted from the hall, but I didn't try to eavesdrop. Hopefully she was talking some sense into him.

Graham's gaze fixed on his plate as he took giant, teenage-boy bites of his sandwich. It was obvious from his blazing red ears that he was fully aware of my parents' conversation about him. Having been the subject of bullying my whole life, I knew exactly the shame he had to be feeling. Although I didn't know what he had done, I felt awful for him. I offered a lopsided grin. "My parents are sort of annoying."

"It's okay." His voice was even. Void of emotion.

I stared at his lowered lashes. They were beautiful, the way they curled right at the tips. My mom would disapprove of my asking, but I could hear she was still distracted with her own conversation. I swallowed, pulling up my courage. "Can I ask what you did that is making my dad so crazy?"

He raised his lashes, letting his eyes hit mine. It sent a chill down my spine. I wasn't sure if I was excited or scared when a cold rush bellowed into my extremities. "You don't know?"

"How would I know?" I rushed to whisper back.

"I'd assumed someone would have told you by now."

"No, I think my parents are protecting me from it." I covered my mouth with my palm, speaking through it. "Whatever it is." I waited for him to say something, but he didn't, so I added, "I won't judge you. I get beat up every day in school. I know what it's like to be made to feel shame."

Having practically inhaled his sandwich, he brushed off the last of the crumbs on the center of the plate while he stole a look down the hall, before starting in a whisper, "I don't care if you judge me. I don't care about people." I started to interject, but he kept talking, "My mom's not real present in my life. The court called it neglect. Never met my dad. I've pretty much been on my own my whole life. Nobody cared or said anything because I was good at school, and I could play football."

He coaxed his head to the side, as if he was giving me a chance to let that info dump simmer. I didn't flinch. He went on, "Quarterback, running back, I'm good at it all. My biggest problem was I went to the high school on the wrong side of the tracks. However, since I played ball there, the team won three state titles—for the first time ever. I became their little small-town hero. People started being nice to me, despite my address. But I don't care about any of them. I didn't play football for them or the stupid town. I did it for me.

I had a plan. I'd get a football scholarship for college. Since I had no other means to pay for college, it was pretty much my only option to have a chance at a normal life. However, with the economy the way it is, the city decided to cut school budgets. Our little south-of-the-tracks school got hit the worst. They completely cut the budget for all extracurriculars, including football."

His eyes explored mine while my heart drummed fast against my rib cage.

"I should add, the other school—on the right side of the tracks—got money for a new stadium. They said it was because the boosters were fundraising, but it infuriated me. I tried to transfer, but the zoning committee wouldn't let me. They argued everyone would want to do that. I didn't care about their fancy stadium. I'd play football in a dump yard if it meant I could play. It was unfair. I didn't choose to live where I lived—" His voice cut off. A loud shuffle from down the hall boomed.

We both turned our heads as my dad stomped upstairs. His footsteps echoed, sending out ripples of warning, signaling to us both that even though he was going upstairs, he would still be *just upstairs.*

Mom padded down the hall and softly said, "I made up the couch for you, Graham. You can sleep there." Then she looked at me with a serious face. "Elinora, I need you to come upstairs now. Your father wants you to be in your room for the rest of the night."

Graham immediately tucked his gaze on his plate again. I blew out a frustrated breath. There was no point arguing. I noisily pushed my chair back, tagging behind my mom without even saying goodnight to Graham.

I was outraged at the way my parents were treating Graham. They were being bullies. And who cared if they were being gracious to let him stay here? They made it obvious he wasn't welcome. I had seen that look of shame on Graham's face so many times in the mirror that I couldn't help but take his side. I wanted to run back downstairs and apologize on behalf of my parents, but they'd hear me. We'd both get into trouble. With the way my parents acted, they'd more than likely place the blame on Graham. I didn't want to make his life worse. So, I gave up and went to bed.

The next morning, I expected to find Graham sitting in the kitchen eating breakfast, or maybe watching a video in the living room. The downstairs was quiet, and no one was around. The sound of the lawn mower alerted me, and I glanced out the window. Graham was pushing our mower. My dad had to be behind this weird indoctrination.

It only took me another moment to find my dad perched on a folding chair in front of the garage. His chair was facing Graham, but next to him, lying on the ground, was a pile of dead pheasants. They were orders from his clients. He did hundreds of them yearly, but he never made his craft this public before. Nor had he ever stacked all his dead animals up like that! He'd work on one at a time, leaving the other carcasses in his deep freeze. He was clearly sending a message to Graham. This had to stop. I rolled my eyes.

He had completely lost his marbles.

The front door opened loudly, and Mom carried in too many grocery bags strung on her arms. I accepted a couple bags without asking. She shot me an appreciative look, but her lips were tightly pinched, hinting her nerves were still piqued. I knew better than to ask about Dad. Instead, I asked, "Have you heard from the social worker?"

"I was just on the phone with her." Mom dropped the rest of the bags on the kitchen floor, then flexed her wrists a few times before remembering her train of thought. "Um, she isn't having any luck. I told her Graham could stay another night, if needed. I don't want to think about telling your dad what I agreed to." Her face turned to the window, and her eyes followed Graham pushing our mower. "That poor kid." Her lips folded in as she turned back to her groceries. In a forced change of subject, she pulled out a package of chicken. "I'm making chicken wings for dinner, so don't get full of snacks."

Chicken wings were Dad's favorite. She made them every Sunday during football season, as she was one of those people who always used food to try to please people. The wings were evidently some sort of peace offering, but I wasn't stupid enough to think they'd work. I did what I thought would be best for Graham and went upstairs to hide in my room until my mom called me to come back down.

Dinner was awkward, with a lot of silent chewing, and we got to eat at the regular kitchen table, so, other than the chicken we were eating, there weren't any dead animals in the room. That was progress. When my mom started to clean the dishes, I went back upstairs, figuring that was best.

I had every intention of shutting off the light, climbing into bed, and staying there all night, like the daughter my parents wanted me to be. As I reached under my pillow, my hand met something hard. A book.

I pulled it out without even having to look at it, knowing it was our notebook. He had a message for me. He must have snuck it up here when he had excused himself to use the bathroom. I leaned over to my nightstand and clicked on my lamp. My eyes fled back to his book. It wasn't a message, but a poem.

From out of the dark, in front of me is a stranger
Opposite the moon-lit sky.
Now he's beside me, a shadow
Of which is my only friend.
Aside this stranger,
I don't know what to do but stand.

My brow bent down, and I reread his words slower. Graham had to be lonely. At least I had Bre, but it didn't seem like he had anyone. His words described his state of life beautifully.

I stretched out, laying on my stomach, and dug deep until I found something.

If you ever need a way to walk,
Come with me while I talk.
Together, we fight off the demons.
I don't need excuses or reasons.
Together, we glue back the pieces
While I take all your shirts made of fleeces.
I will go to war with you.

I waited an hour after the house was completely quiet and sneaked back downstairs. With my heart pounding in my ribs, I tiptoed through the hall, not even turning on one light. When I made it into the living room, I stopped in the doorway. The streetlight created a soft beam through the picture window and landed on Graham's resting cheek. The way he was lying, with his leg bent up in a ninety-degree angle, told me he wasn't sleeping.

"Graham," I whispered, risking a few steps forward so I could speak quietly. "I got our book." He sat up but remained silent. Even though we were alone, I never took the seat next to him on the couch. A heaviness in my gut begged me to protect him. If by chance Dad came down to find me in here with the lights off...I couldn't even imagine what my dad would do to Graham. Taking a spot on the floor, I slid the book across the floor toward him. "Did you write that today?"

"I wrote it last night." He took it, immediately concealing it under his pillow without even glancing at it.

"I understand it."

His chin lowered. Even in the darkened room, I knew he had lowered his lashes. "You'd better get back upstairs before you get in trouble."

My heart pounded so loudly I wouldn't have been surprised if my dad heard it upstairs and came barreling down. I chewed the side of my cheek, watching the doorway for shadows. There was nothing. "Do you want me to go back upstairs?"

Silence.

After a beat, he said, "Nobody ever cares what I want."

"I care."

I found myself scooting closer so I could see his expression. Now an arm's length away from him, I studied his face. He held his somber expression, but something was off. Like the I-don't-give-a-crud-about-anything shield he always wore was *down*. "What do you care about?" He snipped back at me, but I didn't take offense.

Time wasn't on my side, and I pressed on. "I want to hear the rest of your story."

"Nah." He looked away in a dismissing manner. "It's a good thing I never got to finish it, because you wouldn't want to know."

I reached forward, lightly touching his forearm. "I promise I won't judge you."

"Whatever. If you insist." His words blew out in the mutter. A seed of anxiety sparked in his eyes as he leaned forward. "So, I told you about how the football team I played on had won three championships but got their funding canceled."

I nodded, keeping my eyes glued to his faintly lit face.

"And that the rich team across town got a new stadium, but they wouldn't let me play."

I nodded again.

He planted his dissociated stare on his face and peered out the window. "I couldn't fathom how my address was making—breaking—my future. And nobody cared. I would have been an asset to the other team. Nobody even wanted to see me try out. A week earlier, I had been a town hero. Then I was nobody, but—"

"But what?" I couldn't wait for him to finish. My heart was beating in random parts all over my chest.

"But I got a lesson the hard way in learning that life isn't fair. Even if you think you can change it, don't try, because people want to keep it unfair. They like being comfortable. As long as the uncomfortable things stay out of their sight."

I swallowed, but it was more like a gulp. I think Graham heard it, because his eyes deflected from his stare out the window, and he turned toward me. "I don't regret it. I'd say I regret the consequences that it had on my life, but people must start standing up to the system. There is no reason I shouldn't have been able to try out for that other team. It should have been based on merit. I'm not bragging, but I was better than every single one of those guys. They said it was something about conference rules, because I didn't go to school there, but they wouldn't let me. Who even makes these rules?"

If he didn't tell me what he did soon, I'd pass out from holding my breath. "Just tell me."

"After doing things their way—appealing to the zoning committee, writing letters, getting signatures on a stupid petition—I did everything I could think of, and they kept coming back to my stupid address. It had nothing to do with how I played football. It was a dumb idea, but I wasn't planning to hurt anyone. I wanted to make a statement, so I grabbed a baseball bat and jumped the fence of the new arena and smashed up as much as I could."

Gasping, I held my chest.

"The town actually rose up, defending me, and I would have gotten away with it." I was so dumbfounded that I couldn't emit a sound. He went on, "The social workers came snooping and saw my house, and how my mom was never home. They called it abandonment. I got pulled into foster care while I had to wait on the court stuff to settle. The judge saw my straight A's and football record and had mercy on me. He said I didn't have to go to juvie, but I needed a safe place to live. That's why I got sent here." He tossed up a shoulder.

My mouth hung open, but nothing came out. I closed it and tried again. Still nothing. He dropped his gaze, now picking his thumbnail. "Everyone said I got lucky getting off, but there's nothing lucky about my life."

I understood.

I understood what my parents were arguing about. My mom was torn, knowing none of this stuff—at least his home life—was his fault. Did he break the law? Yes. Did I judge him? *No.* People failed him. I reached my hand, touching his arm again. "I'm sorry, that—"

The hall light turned on, and I tucked down on the floor, flattening to the ground military style. Graham threw a blanket over himself as he rolled over, pretending to be sacked out. I speedily crawled around the corner, desperate to get out of view, only stopping when I was behind the corner chair. The only way I'd be busted now was if my dad pulled the chair out—which I wouldn't doubt he'd do.

We waited, listening to the steps in the hall pace up and down forever.

I don't know how many trips the footsteps took up and down the hall, but it was clear it was my dad, because they were stomping. Mom was light-footed and wouldn't sound like that even if she were dragging a dead body behind her. Then the front door opened, the lights switched off, and the door shut. He was gone. It had to be hours past midnight. I assumed the place he was going had to do with getting Graham gone.

"You'd better get back upstairs," Graham said sternly.

"I don't want to." My words were soft yet brave in conviction. In a weird way, I hoped to plant a seed of trust, showing him I was on his side. I crawled out from my spot, returning to the floor next to Graham. Although I was cautious, I also felt comfortable. "I want to talk some more about you."

"I'm not that interesting," he grumbled. "I did one stupid thing that will define the rest of my life."

"What happens after you leave here?" I had always known he was only here to visit for the summer, but I had never entertained the idea that the life he had to go back to… wasn't worth returning to. My heart slammed against my rib cage. Everything felt wrong.

He shrugged, his face blank as if he was completely stumped. "The state will find a 'suitable' place for me. Foster care at best. Juvie at worst. Judging from the amount of time it's taking them, my guess is juvie. Nobody wants a poor kid from the wrong side of the tracks with a criminal record."

I shook my head, feeling angry at all the people who failed him. "It's so unfair."

"Right. I already covered that. They don't care if they don't have to look at the person losing."

"But what about college for you and all that?"

"I probably can't get in with a criminal record. I've heard I might be able to have that stuff erased from my record, but I have no idea how. It's not like I can afford a lawyer to talk to anyone about it. If I could afford college, I'd love it. I love school and I'm really good at it—the academic part, anyway. The people part sucks. At least back there. I never want to go back."

The hollow tone of his voice was a sledgehammer to my heart. "If you could go anywhere, where would you go?"

His eyes clouded, brimming with an air of adventure. "I've heard Vermont is nice." He tipped his head toward me. "So, your turn to tell me about your issues."

I narrowed my eyes, seeing how trivial my little high school drama had been compared to his life. There was no way I could even bring it up. "I don't have any issues like that."

"You said you get bullied at school. How come?"

"I can't—"

"It's only fair."

I flashed my gaze heavenward—this would sound so lame after his confession—but I gave in. "I'm chubby. So, you know, fun to pick on."

His brow plummeted from my anticlimactic answer. "That's it?"

"I told you it was lame."

He looked away, but not before I spotted a scowl lace on his face. He murmured to himself, but I could make out what he said. "You're clueless to not see through that deal. You aren't chubby in the way you'd get confused with a Tellytubby. Give it another year or two, and those dumb girls will have to admit they were jealous."

"You think it's funny that I get picked on for my weight?"

"No," he quickly chimed back. "They are dumb because there is nothing wrong with your body. You're beautiful." I searched his eyes, wanting to confirm what he'd just said, and when we finally latched, they were brighter than I'd ever seen them.

Heat rushed across my face. I had never been so thankful I was sitting in the dark. I bit down on my lower lip before whispering, "I'd better get back upstairs."

"I'll see you in the morning," he whispered as I tiptoed out the way I'd come.

The next morning, I was harshly awakened by the sound of the front door slamming. My heart immediately tightened into a hardened shell.

Dad was home.

That was not good.

I quickly dressed and scurried downstairs. Before I made it to the bottom step, I let out a gasp. A police car in my driveway. I grabbed my throat, feeling it close in. "Dad!" I called out in absolute disbelief he could do something so cruel. I fled down the last step, frantically searching for Graham. He was right where the logistical side of my brain knew he'd be. Standing outside next to the cop with his head fixed to the ground.

"Dad," I grumbled. "What did you do?"

Dad peered over at me, his lips curved down, void of empathy. "Honey, Graham can't stay here. If you continue on this path of hanging out with him, he's only going to ruin you."

"Ruin me?" My voice squeaked out, and I fled forward, grabbed his arm, and pleaded, "Dad, don't make this about me. You didn't even ask me."

"It's over." He waved his hands in front of him, as if he was clearing the air of smoke. "He's gone."

My heart pumped even harder with panic. My parents had failed him too. They were like everyone else who preferred not to look. My gaze jerked to my mom, who stood in the corner. When her eyes regarded mine, I saw tears. "Mom, this isn't fair."

She nodded in agreement but didn't mouth a word.

My feet moved without me willing them out the front door, crossing the side lawn in a few long steps, until I stood next to the cop. Graham was headed back inside the house. I trapped his brown beady eyes. "Where are you taking him?"

"He's going to a boys' ranch." The cop offered me a gentle smile, and then shockingly, he said, "Would you like a moment to say goodbye?"

I deadpanned. That cop had to know how unfair this was. Couldn't he stop it? I was flabbergasted, and said, "Yeah, I would."

Jerking his head toward the house with one swift motion, he said, "You can go inside."

I glanced toward my house. My parents would hate this, but I didn't care what they thought. Everything they were doing was wrong. I looked back at the cop. "Just one moment." I rushed through the door of his grandmother's house until I found Graham raiding the cupboards in the kitchen, stuffing the unopened boxes of snack food into his already crammed backpack. Not knowing what to say, as nothing in life should ever be this hard, I blurted out, "I'm so sorry."

"It's not your fault." He offered me a weak smile. We both knew it was a fake smile, and I hated him for pretending.

"I mean, I'm sorry about everything," I rambled with tear-stained words. "Your mom, your school, your grandma, people. Mostly the people who suck."

"I know." His tongue rolled over his bottom lip. "I'm sorry about the kids at your school, too. Though I have a feeling it'll turn around for you soon."

I blinked back angry tears. *How was he getting sent away?* Worse yet, he was using this time to console me. If I were in his position, I would be crying and screaming, and at the very least, breaking a few things. I felt my brow bend down.

Our time was up.

I searched my brain for the right words to say. Something witty to leave him with but I had nothing. My word box was empty.

His beautiful sapphire eyes trapped mine. I didn't move. I was left with a feeling I had never had before—the feeling of wanting to kiss him. I only had another second or two. My dad wouldn't tolerate us being here together. Although I wanted to kiss him, I froze because I didn't know how. I had never wanted to kiss a boy before, let alone actually do it. My mind pulled back to the memory of Bre reading that magazine about kissing rules. Check your breath. *It's too late for that. Morning breath it is.*

Lean forward.

I licked my lips and slowly raised my chin, leaning closer to him, and he didn't flinch. His eyes stayed locked in communion with mine, and his irises softened. When he leaned forward too, I knew he had the same thought I did.

Now what?

Close my eyes.

Now I can't see.

Was that step out of order, because it seems a little hard to navigate things now?

His hand found my chin, causing my breath to hitch in my already tightened chest. He was kissing-close.

Now what?

Something so we don't bump noses. Turn my head?

I didn't have time to think about the last rule, because it was happening so fast. I felt his light touch guide my chin, and I freaked in panic and turned my head, and his lips dampened my ear lobe.

I had messed up!

Jerking back, my eyes snapped open, knowing my face was every shade of embarrassed. "Sorry," I murmured and took a broken-hearted step back.

He didn't resist a humored chuckle. Even though I had messed up our kiss, it had meant something—to both of us. Reaching out he cupped his hand on my cheek. For a moment, I thought he was going to try to kiss me again, but instead he whispered, "I won't forget about you, Chatterbox."

It stung.

I'd only known him a couple of months, and he was heading back to Oregon. I lived in Florida, and we were both a couple of kids. My heart constricted. I didn't want to say goodbye. I hydrated my lips by swiping my tongue over them. "I won't forget you either."

With nothing left to do, we sulked back out of the house, standing shoulder to shoulder. I held my breath while the cop put his arm around Graham. "Come on, son."

Graham climbed into the back seat of the cop car like a criminal. As the cop car drove away, I whispered under my breath, "I'll never forget you." I fought back every tear because my dad didn't deserve to see me cry even though Dad avoided me as if he was disappointed in me. If he only knew I was more disappointed in him.

I was young. Sixteen. Part of my heart went dark when I saw that cop car take him away, knowing how unfair this had all been. *Life was a jerk.*

Five

ELINORA

Present day

Most days, I tolerated my job as a college recruiter even though I spent my life in schools—the place where I had been bullied my entire youth. I mainly had moved on from the trauma of my past. My biggest issue was the starting salary, which averaged out to a measly fifteen seventy-five per hour. I was embarrassed to admit it, but I'd make more money working as a waitress without a college degree. My dad had said, "That's what you get for majoring in English without a teaching component."

How was I supposed to know that some degrees were worthless?

I picked something I loved.

I love to talk, and English is what I speak.

Therefore, it made sense.

Now, I spent my days dressed in a Gator onesie, traveling to every corner of the United States, convincing high school seniors to spend tens of thousands of dollars on a liberal arts degree. It was a clumsy dance with destiny, making me relive my regrets, only this time I got to experience it dressed as a reptilian.

I waved my giant fleece gator hand at the students who avoided my gaze so hard it reminded me of the time my dad had shown up to my homecoming dance as a surprise chaperone. His polyester, palm-tree-printed shirt had been mortifying.

Only another moment later and all the students had cleared out, leaving me in echoing silence. Staring down the empty hall lined with orange lockers and floors littered with forgotten trash, I instantly swapped my cheerleader face for one that was more stoic and let out a sigh of exhaustion. The last bell rang. Cue my lunch break. I wasn't hungry, but I needed caffeine, and I searched my phone for the nearest coffee shop. Bingo. Found one within walking distance, and it was inside a bookstore. Double bingo.

With my life in a different city every week, I was used to spending my lunch hours alone. Travel used to bother me, but it got easier, especially since Bre and I had become roommates. We had gone to the same college, and soon after graduating we'd both found ourselves drowning in the current economy as new grads. We'd done what we always did and pooled our resources together. We'd moved into an old house where I took the master suite upstairs, and she stayed downstairs because she worked as front house manager at an upscale restaurant with crazy hours. Half the time, she never made it past the couch when she got home hours past midnight. I thought about texting to check in but didn't when I remembered she was working the lunch shift. Instead, I headed off on my walk.

Alone.

Mapleton, Vermont had one of those perfectly quaint downtowns. The brick streets made me feel like I had been thrown into a made-for-TV movie. The vast storefront display of books in the window made spotting my destination easy. I yanked hard on the metal handle, and the door wailed in protest. The smell of paper and fresh glue wafted under my nose, slowing my steps as I absorbed the store's ambiance. A huge dark wooden staircase wrapped around the outside wall, leading to the most perfect cozy loft I'd ever seen in a bookstore. It instantly made me want to get lost up there for hours.

If only I didn't have to go back to work.

Taking my time perusing the shelves, I soaked up the spines of the newest releases as I made my way toward the coffee bar on the back wall. The man working at the counter had his back to me, making a drink. I helped myself to a seat on a wobbly bar stool and casually glanced over at the person sitting next to me. A child with dark wavy hair that hung to her shoulders—if I had to guess, I'd say she was maybe four—caught me looking and gave me a little princess smile. I was immobilized. Wild blue eyes set deep behind thick dark lashes—*exactly like ones I had seen before.*

To avoid being rude, I turned away, but quickly snuck another look as the man turned with the drink in hand, placing it in front of the girl. "Be careful, Hadley. It's steaming hot."

"Thanks, Dad." Her little voice was so soft and sweet. If I wasn't already dying inside, I would have melted from her cuteness.

Hadley. A cold wave of recognition tsunamied over me and without thinking, I whispered, "Hemingway."

I didn't have to look at him.

My heart already knew.

My brain rapidly inventoried the facts.

Hadley was the middle name of Hemingway's wife in real life, and he wrote about her in his memoir—*A Moveable Feast.*

I had *once* known someone who loved Hemingway, particularly *that book.*

He had perfect sapphire eyes and dreams of moving to Vermont.

I was sitting in a random small town in Vermont.

Next to a little girl with perfect sapphire eyes.

A little girl who called that man her dad.

"Chatterbox." His voice floated from the side, sending a ping right to my heart. Mustering up all my bravery, I allowed myself to look at him through narrowed eyes.

Terrified because I wasn't ready to see *him.*

I was sucked into a time warp. Suddenly, I was sixteen again, seeing those eyes for the very first time.

I don't think I teleported.

More than likely, I died.

This had to be like a life review.

Yep, I was dead.

For so many nights I had lain awake, wondering what had happened to the boy with sapphire eyes. And here he was. With a little girl. *I never expected that.*

"It's been a long time." My extremities froze. I wasn't sure how I mustered up an audible sound, but somehow it floated out of my mouth.

The smile he gave me was one I recognized, and it twisted my heart into unease. "It has been an extremely long time since I've seen you last." He waved his hand in a gesture to the store. "And you're here in Mapleton. What are you doing in town?"

"Oh." My head sprang up, remembering how strange it was to meet up so randomly. It undoubtedly looked like a stalking situation. I stuttered to clear that up. "I-I'm here for work. I'm a college recruiter for the University of Florida."

His eyes took an obvious sweep over my outfit. "That explains the Gator pajamas."

A modest chuckle plopped out of my mouth. All my usual functioning facilities had been so stunted that I had forgotten I wasn't wearing regular human clothes. Heat washed over my face. "Right." I forced a chuckle. "It's an attention-getting gimmick I use."

"I thought maybe your dad had finally run out of roadkill and started stuffing people." He was obviously making an honest attempt at breaking the ice. I didn't crack a smile. After all these years of wondering what had happened to Graham. And here he was in a small-town, U.S.A. at a bookstore with *a little girl.*

"Ah, not yet," I managed to say. Now that my thoughts were moving fast, I had a hard time not letting them all rush out of my mouth all at once. "So, you're here. You made it to Vermont." I signaled to the coffee bar. "Is this where you live?"

He nodded, not taking his eyes off me. "Yeah, in the town, not at this stool." I laughed politely as he continued, "Vermont was always sort of a fantasy I had. After I got custody of Hadley, I wanted us both to have a fresh start."

Custody.

Why did my throat just go dry?

I cleared my throat, but the rumble I forced seemed to only add more strain. "Well, it's great to see you. I've thought about you…actually. Before. Sometimes." I fumbled for a word that made sense, but all my words were broken. I couldn't take my eyes off his. They were so captivating. More than anything I recalled, and I clearly remembered being mesmerized by them before. In what felt like another life.

"I've thought about you, too." His lashes lowered. "How are you?"

"Good. Good." I nodded and kept going with the only word I could find. "Good. Good." Graham was the only guy who had ever managed to make me speechless. It was his superpower. I'd like to say I hated it, but the truth was that the way it made butterflies dance in my stomach—I loved it.

"That's *good*." He smiled at me in a teasing way.

"And you?" I motioned to the girl next to me, then brought my hand back to pretend to scratch an itch on my cheek. "You have a, um, a Hadley."

I saw a sparkle that started in his irises and landed on hers. Their connection was so clear and adorable. So undeniably fused and I wasn't sure why, but it brought a single tear to the back of my eye that stung like it was a hundred and fifty degrees.

He had a Hadley.

"Yeah, I have a Hadley," he echoed. His expression was straight and serious, making me wonder about his history and hate his history all at once.

Mostly hate his love life.

"You look great." His compliment floated out casually, but it was enough that it sent another spark of heat right to my cheeks.

This encounter was going to exterminate me.

It wasn't that it was Graham—the guy with sapphire eyes.

It wasn't that it was the guy who had been my first kiss.

It wasn't that I was wearing an evergreen alligator pajama onesie out in public.

Okay, maybe it was a little about that but come on.

And it also wasn't because Graham had an adorable daughter with *someone else.* But it had everything to do with the fact that he was the guy who'd kept me awake at night for years, wondering what had happened to him.

And here he was.

The look he gave me seemed to project our past right into the front of my brain. There was so much more in his heated *what-if* stare. And I could have stood in it all day, basking in the memories.

Six

GRAHAM

I wrapped my fingers around the edge of the bar and squeezed, grounding myself in place. I had imagined this day, running into Chatterbox again so many times in my mind. I'd be running out of my executive office in some big city, where I'd bump into her in the hall like some perfect meet-cute collision in which she was lost. We'd instantly know each other and have that moment when we both knew our lives were about to change forever. I'd had that thought so many times, but every time I had a chance to get my life together before it happened.

Until now.

I couldn't be in a worse place as there was nothing impressive about anything I had going on. I'd just bought this dump of a bookstore that barely made enough money for rent. I couldn't even call it a job, let alone a career. I was living upstairs in a one-bedroom apartment I shared with Hadley. *Man—Hadley*. I face palmed. I loved her dearly, but she was never in my fantasy. How would I explain Hadley?

Chatterbox was talking about something. She obviously hadn't changed that part of her personality. It had sort of a coming-home feeling. Okay, not even close to a-coming-home feeling. That would be wholesome. It had an *all-I-wanted-to-do-was-kiss-her-to-shut-her-up* feeling. Ah, now she was staring at me and not talking. Had she asked a question? I wasn't listening. *Think.* "Pardon me?" I asked, doing my best to focus on her words and not on my jetting thoughts.

"I, ah, said you look great, too." Her compliment felt like all the years flashing back. With a goodbye like we'd had so many years ago, it had definitely left me wondering. So many times, I had thought about this—and I didn't want to ruin it again. I just didn't know the right way to *say* it all.

Always a writer, I was better with a pen. Pens were great because they automatically gave me something to fidget with in times like this. I squeezed the counter again, digging for words. "So, are you in town long?" I started in my best casual voice. "Because we should totally meet up for dinner one night to catch up."

Too nonchalant. I can see it in the way she leans back, she's trying to come up with an excuse. Shoot. I should have waited.

"Uh, yeah for the week." She pulled on her earlobe, transporting my mind back to our kiss. "I like to eat," she added with a strained expression.

Every minute or so, her eyes would replant on Hadley, reminding me there was an elephant in the room. Hadley was the best thing to have ever happened to me, and every day I was prouder of her, but it was *complicated*. To make things appear even more complicated—because that's my life—the backdoor opened. Lacy walked in, and her gaze found Hadley. "Hey, hon. Are you ready to go to class?"

Hadley slid off her chair, cup in hand, and followed her, calling back, "Bye, Dad. Love you."

"Love you, too. See you later." I arched my brow toward Lacy, "Thanks. I'll pick them up." They both waved bye, and I waited until the door was closed, all while wracking my brain for possible words to explain this all.

Nothing was ever easy.

Chatterbox's eyelashes fluttered like butterfly wings trying to find their bearings in the wind. It was beautiful and one of those innocent gestures that told me *exactly* what she was feeling. I didn't owe her an explanation, but her discomfort was obvious. "That's Lacy." I motioned to the closed door. "Her daughter is the same age as Hadley, so she helps me by taking Hadley when I'm working."

"Oh." Her lips pinched together. I waited for her to say something else, but she didn't, so I went on.

"I work nights, sometimes at a bar. There isn't daycare available then. She takes Hadley, and, um, she's a friend, and...well, she's married. Not to me." It all sounded so dumb when I heard it out loud. *Stop talking!* She literally came here for coffee, not to hear about my daycare woes. "Thirsty?" I pointed to the bar behind me. She jolted, probably from my lack of segue there, but I held my own and flashed her a smile.

"Oh, yeah." Her eyes fled to the menu. "I'll have a large iced mocha and..." Her words dragged out like she was thinking of the perfect topping. I grabbed the large cup and wrote down mocha and waited for the rest of her order. She was taking forever, and she wasn't looking at the menu anymore. Her eyes had planted on me. "Also, that dinner you asked me to."

I got a rush of some stomach thing. It wasn't butterflies because these were less graceful. Like rhinoceroses stomping all around. I took a chance and wrote my number on her cup, something I'd never done before but I'd seen it in the movies. Then I swallowed that thing in my throat. Strep throat must be going around. I was going to need a doctor before she made it out of here. "I should be done around six."

Her lips slid into a sweet smile. "Perfect." She stood, signaling to the exit. "I need to return to work, but it will be great to catch up."

"I'll make this...for you." I fumbled with the cup like it was my first day at this job and all I had to work with was four left thumbs. She was quiet as she watched me. A bead of sweat rolled down my brow as I finished. I poured more than coffee into that cup, and I was all nerves when I snapped the lid on, handing it to her.

She took one look at the cup with my number scribbled on it. "I'll text you."

She left, rather silently. Not that it mattered how much noise she did or didn't make. I was on full alert and unable to sit, completely dumbfounded. I stared at her back as she hurried down the street. Even though I fought it, it brought back all the hard memories of my youth that I had tried too hard to bury.

Seven

ELINORA

I ducked out of the bookstore, my chest about to implode. There was no way that had just happened. And I was dressed as a *Gator*. Massive facepalm. Only one wasn't enough, so I bounced my head off my palm, and slammed my face again.

And he had a Hadley.

Talk about a gut-punch. I wrapped my arm around my middle, begging my intestines to behave. *How does he have a Hadley?* And she was perfect, a little carbon copy of him but with a happier resting face. I didn't even have a boyfriend, and he had a Hadley. How was that fair?

And to top it off, being a dad made him look even better. Yeah, he was *that* dad. Seriously? I needed advice. I quickly pulled out my phone and dialed Bre.

"Hey," her I'm-about-to-fire-someone voice greeted me.

"Bre," I paused, letting her tone sink in. "How are you?"

"At work. We've been on a three-hour waitlist, and I have no dishwasher. Oh, and one of the guests keeps going out of the emergency exit to vape. He doesn't notice the alarms going off each time he does that. Yeah, it's been a day. What about you?"

"Walking back to work. I ran to get coffee, and guess what?"

"I got nothing. What happened?"

Checking behind to make sure the bookstore door was still shut, I continued to stride forward farther away before blurting out, "You will never guess who was working at the coffee shop."

"Ed Sheeran!" her voice pitched into an excited squeal at the end.

"W-what?" I fumbled, trying to figure out where she was going with this. "Doesn't he live in England?"

"It's a small world, and you called me at work during my lunch rush. It had better be Ed Sheeran."

"No, not Ed, although that would have been epic, and yes, I would have called you." I paused while I pressed the WALK button at the crosswalk. "It was Graham. Remember that guy who lived next to me that summer in high school?"

"Yeah, I remember him." Her cadence was thoughtful. "The one you cried about for months."

"I didn't actually cry real tears." Lowering my chin into the light breeze, I rushed across the road because I had gone over on my lunch break. "We're getting together tonight for dinner to catch up."

"Hmm. Bad idea."

"I know! It's a horrendous idea," I squealed as all my emotions burst. "I just died thinking about it. I should be planning my funeral."

"Is it a date?"

"I don't know." My heart rate ticked up a notch. "He never *called* it a date."

"Unless you want to get your heart crushed again, I would avoid him. But I also know you're stubborn and won't listen to me. I have to work until close tonight, but text me later to fill me in on all the ways he broke your heart again this time." She was giggling by the end of her rambling, tipping me off to her sarcasm.

"It's just dinner."

"You say that now, but just..." Her voice dropped off mid sentence and spiraled into a yell, "Sir, you cannot use that door!" After a rustling noise, Bre jumped back into our conversation. "Call you later, bye." Click.

I ended the call more confused than before. *It was not a date.* He would have called it a date if he had meant it that way.

There are rules about this. *I think.*

The rest of the afternoon, I was chattier than usual, and that's hard to accomplish. Usually when I went to big fairs, kids came with their parents, and I stayed busy because the parents always had questions. Today, I was tucked away in the lobby and expected to catch kids in between classes, and they were avoiding me. Something interesting I noted was that my inner monologue had taken on a bit of a Shakespearean tone as I mused about my current anxieties. *Alas, we are reunited. What will our fate be this time?* It was amusing—to me, at least, and made the painfully slow hours go a little faster. After work, I bolted out of the double doors and almost ran down the street as I texted Graham.

Me: Hey, are we still on for dinner?

Graham: Yeah, I forgot I need to pick Hadley up from an art class at the park tonight. Do you want to meet downtown, and we can grab something while I wait for her?

I let out my breath. *Casual.* Grabbing a bite to eat while he waited for Hadley. Totally not a date.

Me: Perfect. Text me an address.

I waved from where I was sitting on the metal park bench in the little downtown square. Graham had changed his clothes and now wore one of his famous fleece shirts and jeans. He looked like a rockstar, his hair longer than what would have been clean cut. It added to his *don't-give-a-hoot* vibe that I loved about him.

Since I didn't want to walk around as an alligator, I changed, too. If I'd known I would be going out, I'd have packed something that made me *not* look like a grandma. I had planned on relaxing in the hotel after work, maybe watching a movie. All I'd brought was sweats and an oversized floral maxi dress I usually wore as a swimsuit cover. Swimsuit cover it was, with bonus points for having giant magnolias on my butt.

At least it did not have scales.

Much more approachable.

Graham waved his hand, a thin black cord wrapped around his wrist. A man-bracelet of some sort. I'd never thought about a man-bracelet before, but now I loved them. At least on Graham. "Did you have any trouble finding the place?" The annoyed expression he had often worn in our youth was absent, but he still gave off the appearance that he had an edge I couldn't define. Maybe it was the stress of life, but something was unsettled.

"No. Not at all." I tried to find a safe place to focus. His eyes had this immobilizing effect on me, and I couldn't dare look directly at them. I fixed on his forehead. "It was right where you said it would be. Middle of town."

Letting an exhausted sigh fall from his lips, his shoulders visibly fell as if he was letting go of the day's stress. "Sorry you beat me here. I had to close the store," he explained, "I have a few minutes before Hadley's class is over if you want to walk this way." He tilted his head toward the vendors. "There are some food trucks we can check out."

I'd never been shy, but this whole experience brought me back to being an awkward sixteen-year-old. Only now, I had hindsight to see so much more. We synced into step, perusing the boardwalk, and he started the conversation, "What kind of food are you hungry for?"

Hungry. Who's hungry? I had been fighting the *I'm-going-to-throw-up* jitters, and eating was extremely risky right now, but I couldn't tell him that. "Anything, really. Some place that has Cherry Coke." I forced the most agreeable smile I'd ever worn.

"Always Cherry Coke." He smiled at me before tacking on, "I say we grab some burgers from this place." He pointed to the truck a few yards from us. "We can sit in the park. That way, I can keep an eye out for Hadley."

I'd already slid my foot in that direction, forcing myself to ignore the fact that the food truck looked as if I would need a triple-boosted tetanus shot to eat there. I wasn't high maintenance. At this point, I'd do anything to spend this time with Graham. I eagerly replied, "Sure."

When we got our order, Graham led the way back through the town square to a park nestled in between two brick buildings. We shared plenty of polite smiles but not a whole lot of words. I remembered him being quieter, but I didn't recall him being this quiet. It was like my other senses were so alert watching Graham, I didn't have the reserves to talk.

Graham pointed down to the bottom of the hill, where a small group of kids sat in a circle on the ground. All the kids wore matching white T-shirts and seemed organized in that preschool disorderly way. My favorite kid was the one who refused to sit in the circle. He rebelliously lay on his back, several feet away, just picking his nose. His ability to resist conformity even at this young age was truly inspiring.

I turned my attention to my burger, squeezing it flatter, and took a bite just as Graham started to speak. "That's where Hadley does her art in the park. Every Tuesday." We exchanged pleasant smiles, as we both knew I already knew this. "She likes it." His cadence was slow, almost as if he was making up random stuff. "She takes it with the neighbor's kid. On nights I have to work at the bar, or like today when I had to close the store, Lacy takes her. It works out well."

"Sounds like it does." I didn't want to make it more awkward by pointing out that we'd already talked about this. Clearly, he was nervous, too.

"So." He let out his second long sigh of the night. Not that I was keeping count because that would be odd. Sighs didn't seem like a positive thing. It's not like a smile, but it could be worse. Maybe?

"Look at us, sitting in a park, like old times." He gave his signature head shake, sending the wispy strands to the back of his head, clearing his face.

"Wow, yeah." I checked behind me as if I was making sure I was in fact, sitting in a park. "Sort of like old times." *Except you have a kid.*

"Tell me about your life." He gestured toward me. "You're obviously still in Florida. Married? Kids? How do you like your job?"

My breath came out in a whistle as I instantly triaged those questions in order of importance, assigning the whole "married" inquiry in flashing neon letters in my mind. "That was a lot of questions."

"Sorry." His lashes lowered, hooding all the beautiful sapphire hues under them, the way I had always loved. I marveled at how so much time had passed—*ten years*—but I never forgot how his somber expression had such an effect on me. "Feel free to ignore any question you don't want to answer."

"It's fine," I said in my best breezy tone. "Yeah, I'm still in Florida. Not married. No kids. The job is...meh." I'd never understood how he was the only person who had this ability, like he could see all my secrets with the simplest gaze.

One of his brows took a northerly hike. "Just meh?"

"Well, I get to talk all day, so that helps, but I have a hard time telling people to spend thousands of dollars on a slip of paper that may only net a job that pays fifteen bucks an hour. It works out if they can go to med school or something. Other than that, I don't know if they will see the reward."

He chewed, and I kept right on talking. "I get to travel, which is nice. And again, I basically get paid to talk all day. In that sense, it's a dream job. So, it's your turn. Same questions. College? Married? Uh, you have Hadley, so yes to kids. How do you like your job?" I rushed out all the questions, even faster than he had with no spaces between words.

"No college," he promptly answered. "I dropped out of high school, actually." He rubbed his chin with his free hand, letting his thumb roll over his jaw several times. "I...I didn't do too well after I went to the boy's ranch. I, ah, ran away."

"Sorry." My voice matched his softness.

"We don't have to talk about that." His voice ticked up stronger. "And I'm not married. Never even been close. Actually, I own the bookstore, so it's not just a job. I sort of like it."

I pinned an impressed smile on my face. "Oh, you do?"

"Yeah, I was renting the apartment upstairs and always brought Hadley down to hang out. The old lady who owned it never got mad when we spent the entire day down there, reading all the books without buying them. She had a soft spot for Hadley. When she was looking to retire, she asked me if I wanted it. I hadn't planned on buying it, but it seemed to make sense. It's not a huge moneymaker, but I wanted Hadley to be able to tell her friends her dad did something more than work at the bar." His voice trailed off, and the energy between us seemed to grow thicker. "It's complicated...Hadley."

Sweat coated my lower back so fast, I was glad I'd opted for the breathable swimsuit cover because this conversation was going into uncharted waters. I needed a life jacket. "I'm sure it is," I managed to squeak out.

He ran his tongue over his bottom lip, dropping his voice so much he was almost whispering, "It's not what you're thinking."

"I wasn't thinking anything," I whispered back, not because I was afraid of being too loud. The air in my lungs had run out. I casually placed my palm on my chest, pretending it was comfortable.

What's the name of those breaths they teach you in CPR?

Rescue breaths?

That was what I needed.

In a firmer, more audible tone, he pressed, "You are thinking something, but you're wrong—"

How was it possible for my lungs to clench even more? I didn't want to hear about his love life—past, current, or future. I didn't have the stomach for it. I was being insanely immature. We were both adults. Of course, we had lives, but the thought of him loving someone else hurt deeply. Before I passed out, I cut him off, "No, I have—"

"Hadley is my sister," he blurted out, speaking over me.

My brows stitched together. That didn't match my memories. "She called you." I paused, still confused but pressed forward in the quietest voice ever, "*Dad*."

His gaze angled away from mine, morphing into his dissociation stare. "The state restricted my mom's parental rights to Hadley while she was pregnant because of her record of neglect. They were going to place Hadley in foster care, but she refused to sign consent for adoption." He scowled as he dug his teeth into his bottom lip. "Adoption to a permanent family would have been one thing, but I couldn't let her live foster care life, too. I had just gotten out of it. It tore me up to think of her entering the system so young. She was only a baby. I don't know. I had no idea what I was doing, but my mom agreed she'd only sign away her rights to me. I actually just officially adopted last summer even though I'd had her since she was born. It was expensive, and I had a lot of things I needed to take care of first. I still can't believe the state let me get this far into the process with my record. Sometimes I wake up at night in a cold sweat, scared to death because I can't believe I'm a dad."

"Um, you are right." My jaw dropped so low, it had to have come unhinged. "I wasn't thinking *that*."

"Sorry." His lashes lowered to the ground. "I would have told you at the store. I wasn't trying to be misleading, but Hadley was right there, and she knows she's adopted, but she doesn't really understand the more complicated stuff."

"You were right. Totally complicated."

"It's not something I can blurt out. I don't care if people judge, except for her sake, I guess." He shrugged his shoulders. "Whatever. I'm sure I'm not making any sense."

"You are."

"I bet you think I'm crazy for taking custody of a child."

"No, I don't. I think you're brave."

He squinted as if the sun was too bright. It felt like more of a protective maneuver than anything because the sun was already going down for the night. Even though he was putting up a small guard, the fact that he'd opened up to me at all sent a whirl of flutters into my gut. That was the thing with him. Just when I thought I knew him, he surprised me with another mind-blowing layer! What single man would put themselves in this position? Sure, he was doing well for his circumstances, but man did it take a lot of heart to take on a child.

He abruptly stood and arched his neck toward the circle of kids. "It looks like they are wrapping up. Sorry, sometimes they get done early." I scrambled to my feet, wiping my hands on my skirt, and mustered up my best not-disappointed voice. "It was great to see you. Good luck with the store." I watched his body language, wondering if I should lean in for a hug. Even though I was going through the motions of this good-bye, everything felt so difficult—worse than a job interview.

"Hey, Elinora," his voice came out raspy. Combined with the fact that he never called me by my real name, I had chills trickle down my spine. He flashed a look back at the kids before turning his eyes back to me.

"Yeah?" I said in a hesitant way, sliding one foot out, ready to leave.

"This is sort of random. I know you're only in town for a few days, but do you want to go out tomorrow?"

"Like this?" I stammered, holding up my half-eaten cheese-burger, eyeing the glob of ketchup starting to ooze out the side of the bun, threatening to drip. Ope, too late. It splat-tered on my sleeve. I didn't have a napkin handy, and it was oozing down my arm, staining a trail.

Just once can I be glamorous?

"No. Not like this." He let his amusement linger in his smile. "This was me picking up my kid."

"Right, I knew that." My eyes were still locked on the ketchup, pleading for it to not embarrass me.

"I can get a sitter. We can go somewhere, just the two of us."

"I, uh, a—"

"It's cool." His eyes fled back to the group of kids. "If you don't want to. Hadley is by herself down there, so she might be getting nervous if she doesn't see me." He took a step backwards down the hill toward Hadley.

"No," I called after him. "I didn't mean I don't want to, because I do—"

His lips slid into a grin, and before I could finish, he said, "Great. I'll text you tomorrow." He motioned away with his head, adding, "But I need to go, because she panics easily." Then he turned and jogged down to meet Hadley.

"Okay," I said to myself since he had already left me alone with my racing heart. He'd said *go out.* That's a date, right? He needed to be clearer. I could use some footnotes.

Date or not, I felt a pull that needed to see him again because he was...*Graham.*

Eight

Elinora

I stared at the four neatly folded gator onesies and three pairs of sweatpants in my suitcase. The only clothing stores in this small town had closed at five, the same time I got off work. Hard lesson learned: Always pack a little black dress. You never know who you'll run into. I pulled out my sweatpants, and hoped it worked for whatever Graham had planned. Then I called Bre. "Tell me not to go," I blurted out as soon as she answered.

"Don't go!" She added a dramatic accent.

I paced between my hotel bed and the tiny window. "Not like that."

"What exactly are you not like *thating*?"

"I have a date. With Graham." The mere mention of Graham's name sent a flutter of nerves in my stomach.

"Didn't you already do that last night?"

"That wasn't a date, but I think this is."

"And you don't want to go?"

"Oh, no," I rushed. "I want to go, but I'm freaking out."

"It's just a first date. Those are usually boring anyway. You could probably skip it."

"I can't skip it."

"Okay, then don't tell me to tell you not to go. I'm confused here. What am I supposed to be telling you?"

My phone vibrated with a text, sending a shockwave of adrenaline right through my arm.

Graham: I'm downstairs in the lobby.

I could die. That would be easier than this.

I returned my phone to my ear, struggling to hold it steady while I blurted out, "He's here. Gotta go."

I ended the call and bolted out of my room to the elevator. My inner monologue was rambling like a ninety's gameshow host. *Tonight, I embark on one of life's most curious adventures. Am I going on a date or not?* I swallowed as a chill trickled down my spine.

When the elevator opened on the bottom floor, Graham stood in front of it, wearing relaxed jeans and a nice button-up shirt. My heart constricted, seeing him waiting on me with his hands neatly clasped behind his back. His lips curled up into a flirty grin, making my toes curl. "Hey, *you*."

I flicked my hand up to wave, and the quibbles in my gut rumbled. "Hey...how are you?"

"I'm good. And *you*?"

"Good." I clamped down on my bottom lip, fighting the urge to nervously ramble. "What's the plan for tonight?"

"Good question. There isn't much going on, but the town has this outdoor movie in the football arena every week. Tonight, they are playing *Titanic* in celebration of the twenty-fifth anniversary of its release. I thought we could check it out. Does that sound okay?"

I sucked back a whole lung full of relief. I was so glad it was nowhere fancy with my sweatpants, but fancy or not, I was going to suffer dearly for this. The last time I'd allowed myself to crush on him, it had taken...well, how long had it taken me to get over him? I slammed my gaze to the heavens. *Never.* I still lay awake some nights thinking about his smile. Going out on an actual date was only adding gasoline to this fire—the premium stuff I can't afford. *I shouldn't do it.* Now was the time to run before my heart realizes what was happening. "Um, it sounds wonderful...*but—*"

"Nah." His lips slid into a teasing grin. "No buts. Just relax." His gaze paced my outfit, "It looks like you are taking relaxed to the next level."

"Right." I spurted out nervous chuckles, as my chin tightened into tiny quivers. Relaxing was not as easy as it sounded, especially when I stood next to him.

He signaled to the door. "I have my car, but the movie's just around the block. We might as well walk. I don't think we'd get closer parking, anyway."

"That's fine." We moved in unison out the sliding glass doors, falling into an easy stride on the sidewalk as I set my focus on the sunset, teasing amber and rose tones.

Graham's phone vibrated, and his jaw twitched, as he pulled out his phone and started texting. "Sorry." He spoke with his eyes glued to his phone. "I know this looks rude, but the babysitter is wondering if Hadley can have an extra dessert."

"No problem." My heart swelled with warmth, seeing him dote on Hadley. He was the last guy I'd ever expected to be a single dad, but seeing him care for her made him so much more attractive. And he had clearly been hot before. We slowed our steps as we approached the arena and the line of people curled around the tiny ticket booth, stretching out to the sidewalk. "This must be it, huh?"

The line moved fast, and we shuffled our feet up to the front where we met a lady wearing a huge 1900s-era crimson hat with a giant white feather stuck in the side. Her theatrics instantly made me nostalgic, and ready for the movie. "Two tickets, please." Graham held up his phone, readying to swipe his Google pay.

When it cleared, the red hat lady pushed two paper bracelets under the window and pointed to the left. "Top row is all that's left. Take any seats you can find in section D."

"Thank you." I took my bracelet, strapping it on as we meandered out of line, finding our way up the stairs.

"I didn't think it would be busy, but it looks like we are in the nosebleed section." Graham led the way, weaving through the crowd.

"It's fine." I downplayed how excited I was. I would watch the grass grow in the desert if it meant we could hang out. I stayed by his side until we got to the very top row and plopped down on the metal bleacher, sandwiched tightly together between two families.

"I hope you didn't want snacks," Graham teased, as we both eyed how far up we were. "I'm not walking down there to get them."

"What?" I playfully elbowed him. "I totally had my heart set on popcorn, Sugar Babies, and a Cherry Coke."

"Oh." Graham shot to his feet. "I'm sorry. I'll run down."

"No!" I grabbed his hand, holding him back. "I was joking."

His head tilted a measure toward me while he continued to hold my hand. "Are you sure?"

"Yes, it was a joke." My smile was wide, and I still couldn't believe I was looking at my best friend again, the man I'd been pining for half my life. Only this time, he was holding my hand, which he didn't drop when he sat back down.

"So," I breathed out right as the breeze picked up, bringing me a whiff of Graham's scent. A light spicy musk that tickled my nose in the best way. "What do you want to talk about?"

"I actually had a memory earlier, and it made me laugh." He cocked his head to the side. "Do you remember the time I borrowed my grandma's car to teach you how to drive?" We shared one of our secret smiles, the one that was always emblazoned in my mind because I loved it so much.

"Do I ever." The question instantly threw me back to that summer. Frankly, my brain never really left that summer. There weren't many things I could think about that would not transport me. All my younger years had been spent trapped under the strict house rules of my parents, but Graham had been a tease of freedom. "You told me the STOP signs with white borders were *optional*."

He threw his head back, chuckling from deep in his belly, and we shared a sly glance that sent the butterflies in my stomach into a whirlwind. We shared a magnetism that always threw me off kilter. "I can't believe you believed me," he replied without arrogance.

"I didn't have any reason not to. What did I know about driving?" Shaking my head to no one, as I was clearly disappointed in my own naivete. "You're lucky nobody died."

The movie previews flashed on the giant screen in the middle of the arena, and we both hushed. Several scenes into the movie the wind picked up, and I found myself wrapping my arms around my body to stop from shivering. Graham took note of my body language, scooting closer, and wrapped his arm around me. I immediately melted into him. I could have stayed like this all night, but after another few scenes, the wind picked up even more.

Crack!

I startled as lightning split the sky, splicing it open in a freak storm that dumped torrents of rain on us. People jolted to their feet, covering their heads, and ran to the safety of their cars. Another low rumble of thunder echoed so loudly that my bum felt the vibrations on the bleachers. "We should not be on metal bleachers," Graham called over the crowd noise as he kept his hand protectively around my lower back, ushering me to my feet. "Hurry, but it's going to be slippery!"

The movie shut off as I linked my arm into his, and we took off together, feet pounding the pavement the whole way back to the hotel. When we were met with the sliding glass doors of the hotel, we bustled through them at the same time, rain dripping into puddles around us. I'd need a change of clothes, and I eyed the elevator, unsure if this was the end of our date or just a pause.

Lightning crackled behind us, and Graham's phone vibrated. Before I could ask if he still wanted to salvage our date, he winced at his phone screen. "It's the babysitter. I'm sure Hadley's freaking out." He quickly put the phone to his ear while he paced a few feet away from me. I caught enough to know he was trying to calm down Hadley. After only a moment, he reassured her he'd be right there. When he turned back to me, I was already prepared to say goodnight.

"It's fine." I flicked my hand up, ready to wave goodbye. Tears pricked the backs of my eyes. It was so stupid to be emotional about this. It was a stupid date. *A stupid date we never even had a chance to enjoy.* "She needs her dad."

He locked his gaze on me. "I'll make it up to you."

"Really, it's fine. Nobody even saw that storm coming. It's not your fault." I waved my hand, gesturing out the door. "I'm soaked anyway—and cold. I should get a warm shower." I took a step back, proving I was already over the date.

"I'll get ahold of you tomorrow?" His voice ticked up in pitch at the end, ending his statement more like a question. Lightning flashed again, followed by a huge crack of thunder.

"Sure." I forced an *it's-fine* smile. "Go to Hadley."

"You're the best." He spun on his heel and ran out the door. As much as I wanted this date to happen, it seemed like our timetables couldn't match up. It was exactly what had happened when we were younger. Had we been allowed to spend time together, I didn't doubt he would have been so much more than a one-summer crush. I was leaving in two days, and we had yet to make any real foundation of anything. History was repeating itself. I sarcastically stuck two thumbs-ups in the air as I dragged my feet to the elevator, mocking myself. "I'm the best."

Nine

GRAHAM.

I propped Hadley up on an oversized pillow on the couch and snuggled next to her as the beginning scenes of a Veggie Tales movie played. Hadley's eyelids sank lower with each blink, and she was peaceful. Now that she was settled my mind went straight back to Elinora. She looked so disappointed when I left. I couldn't leave things the way they were. With Hadley entirely distracted now, I texted her.

Me: Sorry about the freak storm.

Elinora: It's not your fault. If they had seen it coming, they wouldn't have even started the movie. It came out of nowhere. How's Hadley?

Me: Better now that she's home.

Me: Thanks for understanding.

Elinora: Of course.

Me: This wasn't what I planned.

Elinora: I know.

I tapped my thumbs on the edge of my phone, fidgeting while I tried to find the words to explain how I was feeling. I didn't want to come off desperate, but I wanted her to know how I felt.

Me: I'd love a chance to make it up to you. Would you want to have a redo?

Elinora: I don't know what I want.

My brows knitted together as her answer was vague and seemed to allude to something else.

Me: Everything okay?

Elinora: Not really. I've been really flustered since running into you.

My heart sank, as that didn't exactly sound like she was excited to see me.

Me: I know you're leaving soon, but I don't want you to leave with this awkward flop over our heads.

Elinora: Sort of like the last awkward goodbye we had.

Me: Yeah, it's been ten years, and I still can't get that out of my head.

Elinora: Me neither.

Me: I can tell Hadley needs some time at home, but if you want to come hang out with us, you're welcome. Say, tomorrow night for dinner? I can make my famous tacos.

Elinora: Are you sure?

Me: If you are.

Elinora: Text me an address.

My heart ticked up a notch.

It was only tacos.

Yet, it wasn't just tacos. It was a chance to *see* her. If we could spend time together, like we used to, things might feel like us again. *Don't mess this up, Graham*, I muttered as I flicked my phone down next to me. Hadley had nodded off into slumber. I was left with racing thoughts.

I'm one of those guys who only knows how to go too far.

Too far in football.

Too far with the law.

Maybe I was pushing too much with Elinora?

Ten

GRAHAM

Knock Knock. Hadley sprang to her feet, motoring fast to the door. "Dad, your friend is here!"

"I'm getting it!" I beat her to it, slamming my whole body against the door, and paused to catch my breath. Clearing my throat, I straightened my spine, pushed back my shoulders, and turned the knob, smoothly pulling it open.

Elinora stood wearing a t-shirt and gray capri sweatpants, the kind that cinched below the knee and usually had writing on one leg. Hers had a pink heart and an embroidered gator logo. I sucked back a deep breath. Now wasn't a good time to tell her I had a weakness for girls in sweatpants. But really, it didn't matter if she wore a potato sack. *She was my weakness.* She adjusted a paper sack tucked in her arm. "I brought ice cream for dessert."

"Ice cream!" Hadley overheard with her super hearing, pushed past me, rising to her toes, trying to see in the bag. "What kind?"

Elinora reached into the bag, retrieving a pint, holding it down low for Hadley to see. "I bought three different ones. You can pick what you want. First, I have chocolate." She removed the second one. "And I got caramel crunch." She reached back in, pulling out the last one, "I thought you might have a favorite color. Do you?"

"It's pink!" Hadley blurted out, reaching for the bag. Her excitement was evident by the fact that she was now jumping in place.

"That's what I thought." Elinora presented the last pint, "I got pink sparkle berry."

"I want that one." Hadley put her hand on the pink pint, claiming it without waiting for permission, her lips pulling into a mischievous grin.

Before she could snatch it, I grabbed it and held it above her head. "Not until after dinner."

Hadley's smile deflated. "Aw, come on, Dad." Her whole body slumped.

"Yeah, Dad." Elinora elbowed me, an amused smile pinned on her lips. "Lighten up."

"Remind me to never let you babysit." I returned Elinora's smile but still put all the pints on lockdown in the freezer. "Now, go wash up." I pointed down the hall to the bathroom, and Hadley obediently disappeared. She was a slow hand-washer, mostly because she loved to make huge soap castles in the sink. It was a total waste of soap and drove me nuts, but today, I was grateful for the habit. It meant I'd have a few minutes alone with Elinora.

Elinora moved a few steps into the room, glancing around the kitchen. "Can I help with something?"

"Everything is done, except for the pico de gallo. I'm making it fresh, but I always have to make two bowls. I like it spicy with extra jalapenos and lots of cilantro. Hadley's is without green things and therefore has no flavor."

"Wow." Elinora let out a light chuckle while her gaze traced my kitchen. "I didn't know you were so domestic."

"It's just pico." I returned to my spot behind the island and resumed chopping cilantro.

"Nah." She turned in a half-circle, scanning the apartment. "Everything. Your place is nice."

I couldn't admit that Hadley and I had turbo-cleaned for a good hour before she arrived. "Were you expecting a dirty bachelor pad?"

"Actually, I was." Her words trickled out with laughter. I wasn't offended because I was too busy trying not to stare at her. The sight of her standing in my kitchen was having this crazy effect on me, making my heart pound harder.

"We have our days when things get out of hand, but I try hard to make our home comfortable."

She nodded, approving. "I'm impressed."

"So." I looked up from my pile of cilantro. "Do you like spicy with green things, or no flavor without green things?"

She waved her hand to the side as if she was physically weighing the decision. "I'll do something in the middle. How about you mix them together for me?"

"I can do that." I took out a third bowl, totally not affected by how her choice seemed to fit right in.

The perfect middle.

Not that it mattered.

Would it matter?

Could it matter?

My thoughts started to ramble, and they spilled over into my words, "Do you want equal parts spicy and non-spicy? Or like one-part spicy and two-parts non-spicy? You can have any combo you want."

Instead of answering me, she helped herself to the stack of napkins and silverware I had set on the counter and set them out on the table. It was cute how she made herself at home. Her lips lifted into a sweet smile. "Are you nervous?"

"Why would I be nervous?" Why did my voice squawk at the end like a dying hawk?

"Because you're using a lot of chatty words, and that's usually what I do—before you tell me to be quiet. I always remember you more comfortable in silence."

She was right. I hated chatter. I wasn't nervous to have her here. Nor was I nervous for her to eat my food—because I was a fantastic taco chef. However, if I allowed myself to be quiet, all I would hear was the sound of my heart slamming against my chest wall. That also wasn't nerves. It was just what she did to me. "I'm not nervous," I answered truthfully. "Maybe I'm like what you said you were—flustered since running into you again." I dared myself to look up.

"It has been flustering." Her words were perfectly spaced and wispy. They were almost like poetry. I should know because I'm a poet.

"I don't think fluster*ing* is a word," I teased, grateful to have something easy to joke about but I steeled my gaze on hers, feeling the magnetism we'd always had.

"There isn't a word that works. I had to make one up." We stayed in an unwavering eye lock, neither one flinching until the patter of Hadley's feet broke our trance.

"Dad, what do you call a sleeping dinosaur?" she asked as she sat at the table.

"Um, a sleepasaurus?"

"No, a dino*snore*." She laughed so hard her nose wrinkled, reminding me of my mom, but not in a sad way. In the sort of way that teased a happy memory and all the joy we could have had as a family—if things had been different. She was my mom's mini-me. Since I also looked like my mom, we all wore the same wrinkled-nose smile. If only my mom would have smiled more. It was an out-of-place thought but having Elinora here was making me remember a lot of random things.

"That's a good one." Elinora moved toward the table, sitting on the edge of her seat.

"I heard it at art," Hadley proudly reported, looking so big in her pigtails and princess pajamas.

"Okay," I cut in as I brought the plates to the table. "I have one non-spicy, non-green, extra cheese." I set Hadley's plate down in front of her. "I have one green, extra-spicy." I set that plate in front of the chair next to Hadley. "And," I set the last plate in front of Chatterbox, "I have one, half-spice, half-non spice, half-green, half-nongreen, and...totally flustering."

"That sounds perfect." Elinora's bottom lip curled under her pouty top lip, as if she tucked it in protectively.

I lowered myself to my seat, dropping a sigh because it felt good to sit after being on my feet at work all day. I picked up a taco, squeezing it together. My mouth watered as I took the first bite, and I chewed through the silence then rushed to start a conversation with the first thing that came to my mind. "What time does your flight leave tomorrow?"

"I have to double-check, but I know it's early."

"Do you need a ride?" I wasn't sure why I offered. If it was early, I wouldn't be able to help her unless I woke up Hadley. She wasn't a morning person, and I'd have to drag her out the door, and things wouldn't be pretty.

"The hotel where I'm staying has an airport shuttle."

Phew, I'd look like a jerk now explaining that I couldn't take her.

"How was work today?" she asked in between bites.

I washed down my last bite with water and swallowed. "It was slower, but I like those days because I get to write."

"What are you writing?" Her questions were quick, like she was doing whatever she could to force conversation.

"I always have several things I'm working on. One day, I'll finish something." I wanted to tell her about our book. I still had it after all these years, and periodically, I'd write to her in it. Over the years, I'd filled about every page, never intending for her to see it because I had been too honest about way too much. Nope, couldn't tell her that. I turned to Hadley, bringing her into the conversation. "What did you do at preschool today?"

She pulled the melted cheese strand out of the top of her taco, slurping it up like spaghetti. "We watched a movie with a cat in it."

"That sounds fun."

"I need water!" Elinora jolted to her feet, fanning her mouth. "Totally flustering on this taco."

"Did I give you mine?" I scrambled to my feet, darted toward the fridge, grabbed a bottle of water, and tossed it to her. "It was extra hot."

She twisted the lid off quickly, and guzzled, swallowing half before coming back up for air. "No kidding. Extra spicy."

"I'm sorry, I eat hot stuff all the time. I don't even taste the spice anymore. Do you want me to make you a new one with just Hadley's Pico?"

"I'm good." She waved her hand in front of her mouth a few more times. "Actually," she gave me a squeamish smile, "I might use your bathroom if you don't mind."

"Sure." I motioned with my finger to the hall and watched her go. When she was out of sight, I brought my eyes to Hadley. "How's your taco?"

"Mine doesn't fluster." She eyed her taco as if she expected it to dance or something. "Is yours flustering?"

Looking down at my empty plate, I hardly remembered eating either of my tacos, let alone tasting them, but they were gone. "Yeah, mine was flustering."

"Hey, Dad." Hadley straightened her spine, sitting up even taller. "Can I show Elinora my room?"

"Sure...if she wants to see it." I dabbed a napkin to the corner of my mouth.

Hadley shot up from the table and ran down the hall, yelling into the closed bathroom door, "Wanna see my room when you're done pooping?"

Shaking my head at Hadley's superpower ability to humble me, I wanted to slide off my chair and hide under the table. Sometimes it was too much. Thankfully, the bathroom door cracked, and Elinora emerged with an amused smile on her lips. "Sure, I'd love to see it."

"Are you coming too, Dad?" Hadley glanced over her shoulder.

I held my breath. This was one of those times where it would appear I was pushing too hard. I hadn't planned on it. Now that it was all unfolding, I also didn't want to stop it. "If you want me to."

"Let's show her what we made." Hadley led the way down the little hall to the only bedroom in the apartment and opened the door, announcing, "Tada!"

Elinora lumbered into the room and her lips parted, but she didn't speak as she turned in slow motion. Truthfully, I was terrified for her to see it. Just as I thought she might not notice it, Hadley exclaimed, "Look at my wish strings!" I closed my eyes, praying it didn't look like I was pushing too hard.

Eleven

ELINORA

My heart thumped against my rib cage so hard, it was going to bruise. A long knotted dandelion string draped from the curtain rod of Hadley's window. The flashback it gave me was so beautiful it hurt. I didn't know what it meant, but the silence in the room told me it meant *something*. "I need to use your restroom again." I tucked back out of the room without looking at Graham, who stood watching me from across the hall.

"Are you feeling okay?" Graham called through the bathroom door. His words were hesitant at best.

"I'm maybe fine." I tried to pace, but the tiny bathroom was only a few feet long. I dropped to sit on the edge of the tub while I drove my thumb nail between my lips, biting down hard. Over and over while his footsteps traipsed down the hall and back again.

He must have had his face pressed to the door when he asked in a quiet voice, "Are you sure? I can get you some medicine?"

My nail broke into my mouth, and I spit it in the trash. It was a disgusting habit I never let anyone see, but it was my lifeline to sanity now. "No medicine."

"There's a drugstore right down the street. They are open twenty-four hours and will have anything you need."

"No, thanks." After a moment, his footsteps padded away. I sat on the edge of the tub and stared at the wall. *Why is this affecting me so much?*

It didn't make sense for a guy I'd known for the shortest summer in my youth to have stayed in my head all these years. Nor was it explainable that we'd run into each other without even trying, that we both got so flustered when we were around each other.

And the dandelion strings . . .

It meant he hadn't forgotten me either.

I ran cold water in the sink and splashed a big wave on my face. My shoulders cringed as my mind alerted and reset, freeing me of my fluster. With brave fingers, I opened the door and emerged to find the bedroom light dark. A soft clattering noise came from the kitchen.

I tiptoed down the hall and found Hadley snuggled on the center sectional couch with a pink blanket, watching a cartoon on the older model TV in front of her. Her eyelids drooped as I snuck past the living room to join Graham at the sink, where he was washing the dishes. "Are you better?" He kept his eyes low on his scrub brush, moving it in a circle on a plate.

I walked until I was standing shoulder to shoulder with him. "I don't know."

"You can sit down if you want, or I can take you home." A look of concern washed over his face as he turned and squared his body with mine.

My gut fell into a freefall. "I'm not sick." His gaze softened but it never wavered. I didn't dare move. If I did, I wouldn't stop until I was in his arms. The image of Hadley's room and the dandelion strings slammed into my brain. "When did you do that?"

"That one we just made before you came over. That's why it's not dried up yet, but we make them all the time. Over the summer, whenever we'd go to the park, I'd usually bring my book to read. She'd sit next to me and have something to say. I never got much reading done—and it always reminded me of another time I tried to read at the park. I'd give up. Since I had no idea what to do with a little girl, we made dandelion chains together." His voice trailed off at the end, but his lips curled brilliantly. "There's been a lot of moments that reminded me of you over the years," he stated firmly, making me believe he was sincere.

My breath hitched in my chest, but I wasn't ready to be that honest with him about how much I had thought about him. Instead, I turned toward the sink. "Can I help with the dishes?" I opened the cupboard in front of me, and I started moving dried plates to it. We fell into a synchronized pattern of washing and drying, and the conversation finally seemed to get easier. "It's amazing to see you with Hadley. You make it look easy."

"It's not easy." He shot me a telling look. "But somehow, we keep plowing forward. At this point, I don't know what I'd do without her." He handed me the last plate, but it was a trap. As soon as I placed it in the cupboard, and turned back to him, he pivoted on his foot toward me and dropped his chin. His lips were only a mere inch from mine, and his eyes hung on me, and I was afraid to breathe. After several moments of me holding my breath, he whispered, "Is it weird that having you here tonight feels normal to me?"

Shivers rained down my arms, raising gooseflesh. "I don't think so."

His eyes locked on my lips, and he whispered, "What do you think?"

"I think...I think I'm crazy." My voice trembled in fear of the honesty I was expressing. "It's been years since we knew each other, but my heart stumbles when you look at me like that." I held my chest because it was like my heart was proving a point with this imploding thing. "It makes me want to believe in fate. That's silly, but then I feel like I'm going to go insane—"

"You have every right to go insane. I'm already there. Everything makes sense to me until I think about you leaving. Again, we're being separated by a thousand miles before we even have a chance. This feels like a joke."

"This was all so random, yet it feels right."

"First you said you were confused." He cocked his head to the side, arching one eyebrow above the other. "Now it sounds like you aren't really confused as much as you were just holding back."

"Honestly," I looked up, taking in the deep hue of his eyes. It sent a whoosh of a spark, demanding my heart to pound, screaming in all caps. "I always had a crush on you, and I was mostly holding it together until I saw your dandelion strings."

"The thing is that we're not in high school anymore." He placed a hand on my waist, pulling me to him. The mere friction of his skin put my gut in a twist. "We're in charge of our own lives."

After all the awkwardness, we were finally connecting. I loved this moment with everything in my soul. He took a step closer to me, and now the gap between us was only as thick as a whisper. "I want to be with you, Elinora. I know it's not perfect timing, but is this real for you?"

Memories wafted in front of me, back to the days at the park, the smell of yellow dandelions blooming. It wasn't hard for me. I'd literally had a thing for Graham for years. "It's a thing." I curled my lips into a flirty smile, and I raised my chin up so I could meet his lips with mine. This time I hit my target perfectly. His lips were soft but managed to steal all the breath from my chest. It was the kiss I'd always known we were capable of.

He pulled away first. "You can't imagine how many times I've thought about kissing you like that."

"I might have played a redo of our kiss in my mind, too." My lips still tingled, and I resisted the urge to run my fingers along them.

"I don't want this to change."

"What do you mean?" Ice filled my veins, as I'd thought we were making progress. I wanted us to change. I didn't want to be friends. I wanted more than that. "I thought we were on the same page."

"No." His arms wrapped around me, and he pulled me in closer, dropping a kiss on the top of my forehead. "I want *that* part to change. I don't know what to think about tomorrow. I'd love to say I can visit every weekend, but realistically with Hadley—"

"Right." I gave him a curt nod, my heart plummeting. I hadn't forgotten about the distance between us, but being in Graham's arms was all I'd been dreaming about for years. I wasn't going to force an obstacle when something had clearly brought us back together.

Truthfully, if he'd told me to quit my job and move here so we could be together, I would've called my boss right this second. I'd get a job slinging boxes at a grocery store if that's what it took to bring us together. I bit my lip, knowing it was way too soon to have those conversations, but I also didn't want him to think this was a casual thing for me, a mere convenience while I was here. "Well, I travel a lot for my job, and I'll be back up here in three weeks when I visit New Hampshire. Maybe you and Hadley could come visit?" Dropping my gaze, I slowed my words. "If you want."

"Yeah, that sounds great." His tone was optimistic now, but the fact that he was already pointing out the flaws in our potential relationship left a niggling worry in the back of my head. "Do you have to leave now? Or can you stay to watch a movie?"

"Um." Inside I was doing cartwheels, all my dreams were coming true, but I was also dying a little, knowing this could also kill by degrees. *I was willing to risk it.* "I'll stay."

Twelve

GRAHAM

Three weeks later, Hadley and I packed our suitcases, plus a bag of all her favorite candy she was only allowed to have on special occasions. My gut twisted as I left her with Lacy. Hadley was excited for a sleepover, but I worked all the time, and weekends were our time to hang out. I promised her *next time* she could come with me. If I was going to give this relationship a shot with Elinora, we'd need some time just the two of us. Plus, it was only one night. Elinora would finish work at five, and we would have just a few short hours together. We needed this time. I wished I could stay the whole week, but with the store and Hadley, one night was all I could swing for now.

Juiced on energy drinks, I made the trip alone. I didn't want to risk making her uncomfortable since we hadn't had a real first date. So, I checked into a single room in the same hotel where she was staying. I hoped she didn't have doubts about seeing me again. We had been talking every day, and it was the weirdest sensation to try to describe, but she was the only person I'd ever felt a balance with. I was more myself with her than when I wasn't talking to her. Even though she didn't do anything to push me, just hearing her voice made me want to be more for her with an ease that wasn't present anywhere else in my life. It was the part of my life that didn't make me feel like I had to try hard—loving her was easy. I sat on the edge of my bed, waiting for the time to pass. Finally, my phone lit up.

Elinora: Just getting off work. I can't wait to see you! Me: I'll be waiting in the lobby.

Jumping to my feet, I did a hair check in the bathroom mirror. I had this bad habit of always running my hand through the front of my hair when I was stressed. It made me look like I had serious bed head that could not be tamed. To combat it, I had come prepared with a $6 bottle of drugstore hair gel. I slathered on another layer, vowing to not touch it again all night. Next was the breath check. Even though I'd been pounding Mint Mentos since I got into town, I couldn't risk offensive odors and brushed again.

There. Straightening the bottom of my shirt, I checked for any last-minute malfunctions, and grabbed the bouquet of pink roses I had picked from the grocery store. Once downstairs, I sat on the lobby couch by the window, nervously tapping my foot. If anything, the part that would kill me would be this. I was excited, but until I saw her face, I wouldn't know how she really felt about this. About me.

A white Ford Edge pulled into an empty space right out front, and my stomach flipped. As soon as her door opened, the first waves of her dark hair peeking out, I sprang to my feet with roses in hand. Wanting to meet her outside, I paced forward, eyes searching for her as soon as I sprinted through the door. Her lips curled at the tips, nothing overly excited, but she looked happy.

I hoped she was happy.

She wasn't wearing her gator onesie. Instead, she wore a periwinkle dress that flowed in the light breeze. Her hair fell in beachy waves around her face, in her natural ombre of chestnut and honey blonde. I quickened my pace to catch up, feeling a surge of gratitude that she had agreed to spend time with me. She hadn't noticed me yet., I called out, "Elinora!"

Our eyes caught slowly, a sly hover before her lips sprang into a full smile, and she took the final steps toward me, right into my outstretched arms. I wrapped both arms around her, drawing her into a hug and burying my face into her hair, inhaling her.

She smelled like all the best summer sunsets. The crimson ones that glowed low on the horizon. Her scent emboldened me to press a kiss to her neck, and my toes curled as I did. I didn't pull away from her. I'd waited too long to hold her, and we swayed back and forth, half dancing in the parking lot. When she tilted her head back to look at me, her smile was so large, it was hard to think she'd ever felt any emotion other than happiness. "You're so beautiful." I was surprised my voice didn't croak, but I couldn't take my eyes off her radiating smile.

"I'm so glad to be here." An inexplicable magnetism kept us together, embracing as if we'd been together for years. That had always been the case in my heart, but this was the first time I'd ever acted on it. It wasn't just a physical connection. It was something deeper.

Spiritual.

Usually, I went about my days, running a to-do list through my brain of all the things I should and could be doing. As I stood here, there wasn't anything else I could possibly do other than be here. "I'm glad you're here, too. That's way too many miles for us to be separated."

Pressing my palm to hers, I paused as our hands wrapped together, and my heart skipped a beat. Something so simple, but it felt exactly how I'd thought it would. Like we were meant to be. I dropped another kiss on the back of her hand and grinned as I pushed the roses toward her. "For the prettiest woman in the world."

"I don't know about the prettiest"—she paused to smell the flowers before tucking them close to her chest—"but I am the luckiest."

"I have a surprise for you." I set one foot in front of the other, tugging her toward my car. "Dinner reservations at one of the best places in town. I hope you're hungry."

"That sounds amazing," she cooed wistfully. "I'm starving, but I'm more excited to see you. I sort of would rather stay in so I can get used to looking at you again."

"We have time for that." I opened the passenger door to my car, presenting her seat with a lowered hand. "But not until you are properly fed."

"You just don't want to risk me getting hangry." Even though she teased resistance, she strolled to the car and got in, setting her roses on her lap.

"That too." I closed the door after her feet were positioned inside and raced around to the other side. I was half glad she said she'd rather not go out, because what I'd planned would give us time alone. "Do you still like Cherry Coke?" I reached behind the seat where I had a small cooler and pulled out a cold one I had grabbed just for her. I already knew the answer to her question, but I played coy.

"Drink of champions." She eagerly retrieved the bottle, twisting off the cap. "And perfect timing because I'm super thirsty."

After she took a sip, I shifted the car into drive, and took her hand in mine again, gently squeezing as I anticipated my heart to miss a beat again. Yep. Like clockwork. It's what she did to me. Every time we touched. "Does this feel like a dream?" I steered toward the freeway, barely able to keep my eyes on the road, as all I wanted to do was look at her.

"It feels like…" Her voice dropped off and she stared back at me before tacking on, "Home."

My phone vibrated, and I willed myself to ignore it. It wasn't hard to do at all because I wanted to be present with her. Everyone understood I was out of town today. The only person who'd risk bothering me was maybe…*my babysitter.* "I'm sorry," I muttered as I slid my phone out of my pocket, confirming what I had suspected.

I hit the text to voice.

Lacy: Just letting you know Hadley has a slight fever and didn't want to eat anything all day. I don't think it's much. Maybe her molars are coming in? You're fine with me giving her a little medicine, right?

I voice to text back to her.

Me: Yeah, please. Thank you. Let me know if she gets worse.

I sat my phone in the middle console while stealing a quick glance at Elinora. "She's in good hands."

Elinora tucked a stray hair behind her ear. "If you need to go—"

"She'll be okay." I took a sharp left onto a narrow road, leading to a park I had Googled. It was listed as one of the best places to bring a date. I pulled into a parking spot and popped the trunk.

"Oh." She glanced out her window, eyeing the water around us. "I assumed we were going to a restaurant."

"Remember how you said you didn't feel like going out?" I opened my door and dropped one foot on the cement, staying focused on her. "I figured that would be the case, but I also knew you'd be hungry. So, I packed a picnic." I purposely left off the part that I was flat broke, and spending the weekend away took all my disposable income for the month. She deserved so much more, all the spoiling of a princess, but I wasn't in the position right now to provide that for her. What I couldn't give her in lavish gifts, I planned to make up with creativity. I was trying...

"That sounds perfect." Her eyes widened, reflecting all the light in spirals of happiness. "I can't wait to see what's on the menu." I grabbed the cooler from the backseat, and she followed me to the trunk, where I grabbed my favorite fleece blanket—the one with my high school football logo and state championship title. It was probably the only possession I had left from my youth, as I mostly tried to forget everything about my younger self. Football and Elinora were the only two good things from those days, and now, finally, after all these years, I had Elinora back.

"Can I carry something?" Her hand hovered over the other tote in the corner of my trunk.

"We don't need that one. It's a bag of sand toys for Hadley. I leave them in here all the time." Patting the cooler strap balanced on my shoulder, I walked slowly. "I have everything we need. Let's find a great place to sit."

Making a wide sweep across the landscape, her eyes locked on a grassy hill overlooking the water. "How about there?"

"I'm already on it." I smiled, marveling at how we automatically matched pace with each other, and we strolled right to the center of the hill. After spreading out the blanket, I flipped open the cooler lid. "Care to guess at tonight's cuisine?"

"That's a tough one. Last time we had tacos, but I don't think you'd pack those." She rubbed her hands together, drumming up excitement. "I'm going with sandwiches."

"We have a winner!" I lifted out two brown bags, giving one to her. "Not just any sandwich though. It's my special ham and Swiss sandwich with Dijon mustard and everything but the bagel seasoning."

"How fancy!" Her grin spread wide as she slid the sandwich out of the bag, and she didn't waste a moment digging in. As I sat across from her, I couldn't help but be mesmerized by the way she savored each bite. The way her eyes would close in pleasure, the slight tilt of her head as she chewed thoughtfully—it was as if every bite held a world of flavor. And in that moment, there was something so effortless about her. She was honestly the only woman I'd ever dated who I felt comfortable just packing a ham sandwich picnic for. It wasn't that I wanted to impress her less. *I knew her best.* We knew each other. "Mmm, it's fantastic." She hummed through her chewing.

"Hard to beat the seasoning. It really elevates anything you use it on. Hadley and I eat these sandwiches most days for lunch. We just don't get tired of them."

"Maybe it's the sandwich." She winked at me as she dabbed the corner of her lips with a napkin. "I think it might be the chef."

"Possibly. I have a lot of experience making these."

Her lashes lowered while her face stiffened.

"What?" I pressed softly. She was holding back. "Did you find a hair? It would definitely be Hadley's. She's my sous chef."

"No hair. I've just been wondering something for so long, and I didn't want to ask in a text message." She stretched her legs out in front of her and leaned all the way back until she lay on the ground, resting her hands behind her head.

I had just taken the last bite of my sandwich and stuffed my garbage back into the cooler. Taking a cue, I stretched out next to her and stared up at the sky. A few stars had started to peek out. They glittered in the charcoal sky like scattered diamonds, casting a soft glow for us to focus on. "You can ask me anything."

A longer than usual pause tipped me off that she was changing the tone to something serious, which was only confirmed more by her soft voice when she spoke, "What really happened after you were sent away?"

"What do you mean?" I understood exactly what she was asking, but I needed a minute to think.

"I mean, you dropped off the earth. Your grandma went into a nursing home, and my mom kept in touch. Bertha never said you called or came to visit."

"Right." A knot swelled in my throat. Besides my social worker and my grandma, Elinora was honestly the only person who knew what happened. Well, and her family. I didn't dare tell any of my friends back in Oregon. As far as they were concerned, I had been living my best life on the beach in Florida. I had purposely tried to drop off the earth, because I didn't want anyone to visit me where I was. "I, ah, got brought back to Oregon to a boys' ranch, which was pretty cringe. They made it seem like a huge win that I dodged juvie, but I didn't see any difference. It was a lot of farm labor, and they were pretty heavy on the Jesus stuff." I shrugged. "I hated it and only lasted a few weeks before I ran to the streets. Eventually, I got a job washing dishes at a dive pub. I don't think it was legal for me to work there, but the owner paid in cash, and never asked questions."

"That sounds like torture." Her gaze seemed to dance over the stars for clues to anything else I hadn't said. "I had no idea it was that bad."

"Hindsight diminishes the feelings of torture." My temperament was even, despite how I'd never been able to talk about what happened to me without shutting down completely. The fact that I disclosed this stuff to her did more to tell me how I really felt about her than anything else. "I've, ah, never told anyone what happened to me."

"I'm sorry if you didn't want me to bring it up."

"It's okay. I don't want any secrets between us. Ask me anything."

"Anything?"

"Yeah." I gave her a suspicious side-eye. "Now what?"

"Talk to me about Hemingway."

My brow probably crinkled from the stretch I gave it while I searched her expression. "Why Hemingway?"

"You named your daughter after his wife."

"Oh, that." I nodded, as no one had made the connection before. Most people assumed Hadley was just a trendy name. Again, Elinora knew me more than surface level. "I, ah, love his writing. I studied it for years, and I guess I love his personal story, too—so tragic, not fiction. He loved several wives, but after his last, he died a hermit. Many people thought Agnes, that gal who was his nurse in the war, was his true love. You know, the one they made that movie about? Agnes was the one who got away. His *Farewell to Arms* but not his true love. I would argue his true love was his first wife, Hadley. She was the one true love that never expired."

"It's definitely bittersweet," her voice rolled out dreamily, and I loved the way it sounded. "I sometimes think God hand selects the people with the most beautiful souls to hurt the most, so they can go first to light the way for the rest of us to find healing. Without his heartbreak, he wouldn't have been who he was. If she hadn't died, he might have had a family, worked a trade and the world would have never even heard of him. And look what he's done for the world."

I sighed, resigned. "I used to think about the trauma I went through, and although it was not war, I had to think it was refining me for something bigger. I always assumed it was a football career. Now I don't know. Now I just hope to keep Hadley alive until kindergarten."

She chuckled lightheartedly. "You can't even tell me she isn't a perfect angel."

"She's great, but that doesn't mean I know what I'm doing." I blew out an even breath. As much as I loved Hadley, I struggled daily to be enough for her. I'd never had proper parents. "I think I get a lot of grace because I'm the last person who deserves a kid. It was never my dream to have her. I'm not saying she isn't a blessing. It's just a lot."

"What are your dreams?"

"Honestly, my day-to-day life is so crazy. Getting the chance to get caught up, or even ahead, feels like a dream. I'd love to grow my business for Hadley, but our town is so small that I honestly don't see that happening. I think a better long-term goal would be to change careers and do something more in the corporate world. I hate the idea of being a minion but realistically when you think about adult things like insurance, and all that, I need to consider it for Hadley. Those are my immediate goals. Eventually I'd like to get back to writing. When I have time. If I had a better job, I could use my nights to write instead of working bar shifts."

"That's a good goal. It doesn't seem like it would be that hard."

"What about you? What are you dreaming about these days?"

"Lately . . ." Her voice dropped into a wistful tone as she closed her eyes, a smile playing on her lips. The night sky above shimmered with the now countless number of stars, their light casting a dreamy glow over her gorgeous face. She let out a contented sigh. "I sort of feel like my dreams *might* be coming true."

I was getting used to the way my heart skipped when I touched her, so I could take her hand without holding my breath. "Is this your dream?"

"You already asked me that."

"No, before I asked if it felt like *a* dream. Now, I'm asking if this *is* your dream?"

"Ah." Her lips parted, but she didn't shift her focus from the stars, her chest rising in a deep inhalation. "It always has been."

Dropping her hand, I reached for her face and turned it toward mine, leaning in for a kiss. This time, when my heart skipped, it pained in all the best ways. Kissing her was like basking under a July sunset. I didn't want it to ever end. But I'd promised myself this time I wasn't going to push too hard. She needed to know this wasn't just about a physical connection for me. I planned to invest in her heart first. Breaking our kiss before it became anything but sweet, I dropped another kiss on her cheek to seal it off, and smiled, unable to take my eyes off her. "Are you ready to be my girlfriend yet?"

Her lashes fluttered. "I was wondering how long it would take you to ask."

I gave her my sly smile. "I had to time it just right."

"Of course, timing. I get it."

"Well." I grabbed her hand again, lacing her fingers in mine, playfully dropping kisses on her fingers. "How long are you going to keep me waiting for an answer?"

Tapping her chin with her perfectly manicured finger, she pulled her gaze away. "I need to get the timing right, you know?"

"Stop. I've waited ten years to ask you that." I sat up sharply, unable to take the teasing. I loved flirting with her, but I wasn't prepared to feel as if she might possibly say no. "You have to say yes right now, or I'll implode."

"Oh." She chuckled as she sat up and tucked her arm into mine, pulling her whole body close to me until she could lean her head on my shoulder. A rush of shivers spiraled through my arm, not stopping until it hit my heart at the same time as her words. "It's always been yes."

I was officially done.

I'd dreamed of this moment, of being her boyfriend for so long, and now that fate had pulled this off, it didn't get any better than this. "I will never take you for granted," I whispered before I kissed her forehead, promising myself I would do everything possible to make all her dreams come true because she just made mine come true.

Thirteen

Elinora

We chatted about life, under the stars until the first light of morning. The sun was already cresting over the horizon and at an angle that made me aware I was already running late for the airport. I wanted so badly to stay with Graham. We'd hardly had any time together. It was not fair. I was going to miss him so much, but I reminded myself that work was paying for my trip, and I had to get back on a plane. If I did my job well, they would pay for another trip next month. Sure, if he asked me to quit this stupid job and move to Vermont, I probably would.

No, definitely.

I'd absolutely quit.

However, we weren't there yet. Or maybe he wasn't there yet, because I totally was. From the first summer, I knew he was meant for me. There was no other way to explain how we had been thrown together in our youth, and then accidentally crossing paths now. Oh, and not to mention the butterflies flopping around like tutu-clad walruses. Those helped me to make this decision, too. Sighing, I leaned over and brushed his cheek. "It's morning already. I need to leave."

His dark lashes fluttered as his eyes found their bearings on mine. My heart stilled. The power of his eyes would be studied by scientists one day. His hand snaked over, drawing me into him. "Stay here."

"I wish I could." I had spent countless nights yearning to be near him, feeling the weight of his absence like a physical ache in his chest. But our moment was already over. I couldn't shake off the fear that this reunion would only lead to more heartache. Each time we'd spend together would always end with us returning to our separate lives and I hated this. Taking a deep breath, I wrapped my arms back around him. And in our embrace, a flood of emotions rushed through me—hope, remorse, and all my dreams. It was then that I decided he was worth every hard moment of waiting.

"Well, we can't stay *here* because it's going to get cold in winter, but you can come back to Vermont with me."

"Quit torturing me."

"It would be great." His hand found mine, his fingers trembled slightly as they blended with mine. "You could come to the store with me and work the drink bar while I make faces at you from the stacks."

"Don't tempt me." I squeezed his hand, as he had no idea what his playfulness was doing to my heart. I *would* go to Vermont with him if I felt like he was even remotely serious right now. "I hate to leave, but I need you to drive me back or I'm going to miss my flight. But..." I stressed the T, hoping to keep our parting positive, as I stood up. "I have a week scheduled for New York high schools next month. It would be great if you could drive over."

"Next month is too far away. Why don't I come to Florida in two weeks?" He grabbed the cooler, still sitting where he'd put it last night. "I want to see what your life is like."

I dragged my feet to the car because I didn't want to leave him. "I would love it if you came to see me, but are you sure you can do that with Hadley?"

"I'll make a few calls and figure stuff out." He stopped in front of the car. We stared at each other, not even teasing a smile now. I hated this. I already missed him.

"Actually, I have a family wedding in two weeks. My cousin is getting married. I'm a bridesmaid." I patted his chest. "I'd love it if you could come as my plus one."

"Why didn't you say something? I'd love to go with you. Oh, wait." His lips parted in caution but his smile lingered. "Does that mean your dad is going to be there?"

I cringed through the flashbacks. "He's gotten a *little* better over the years, but I promise my mom will keep him occupied, and there's no taxidermy allowed at the wedding."

"If you can make that a promise, then of course I'm in."

I was all smiles as I leaned in for a deep hug. I tried to memorize every detail—the way his arms felt around me, the scent of his cologne, and the way my heart drummed against my rib cage. It was only going to be two weeks, but the thought tugged at my heart like a relentless ache with no sign of ending. "I won't say goodbye, because I don't want to cry. I'm going to say see you in two weeks."

"Absolutely." He echoed my positive tone and kissed my forehead. "See you in two weeks." With a bittersweet smile, I pulled away, holding his gaze for a moment longer before turning to get in the car. And as I did, warmth filled my chest, reminding me all my dreams were coming true. I just had to be patient.

By the time we returned to the hotel, I had barely enough time to grab my things and race to the airport. I got my boarding pass scanned right as they closed the gate. Something was up with the plane. We sat on the tarmac, waiting, the air smoldering. They couldn't even pass out water for us until we were in the air, and I was getting dizzy. I reached for my phone, texting Graham.

Me: Haven't left the airport.

Graham: R U serious? Did they say how long your delay will be?

Me: They said fifteen minutes, but that was an hour ago.

Graham: Hopefully it won't be too much longer.

Leaning forward, I checked down my row, and everyone seemed to be fidgeting in their seats, and craning their necks around. This was getting ridiculous. I swiped my forehead as I was getting clammier by the minute. Another vibration from my phone.

Graham: I'm looking at flights to Florida.

A smile filled my lips as his dedication made me so happy.

Me: And?

Graham: I don't know if I can make it in two weeks. Things look pretty booked.

Me: Oh, that's okay. If it doesn't work out, we can pick another weekend.

They announced it was time to activate airplane mode on our devices. I was dying at the thought of our plans being thwarted but obediently switched off my phone. When we landed four hours later, I still didn't have a reply.

Me: Hey, I made it home. Did you find a flight?

I took long strides down the corridor, pulling my carryon bag behind me, checking my phone every ten seconds. No reply.

Me: I'm home now. Call me when you get time.

When I passed through the front door of my house, Bre was conked out face down into a throw pillow on the couch. She was piping out little snores. I tiptoed around her, trying to get to my room without waking her. I had a sickening feeling in my stomach. Even if Graham was working, he should have replied with a short text to acknowledge he'd at least gotten my messages. Surely, he'd lost his phone. Maybe Hadley was sick? He'd find a way to get ahold of me soon. Finally, as if he knew my heart couldn't handle the waiting anymore, I got a text.

Graham: I managed to find a redeye flight that comes in early Saturday. I can't wait to see you.

Fourteen

GRAHAM

Two weeks later

"Hadley, wake up, sweetie. I have a plane to catch." It wasn't even bedtime yet, but she'd passed out on the sofa right after dinner. She groaned, rolling over, fully revealing her side profile, and her cheeks looked unusually pink. Waiting for her eyes to flicker awake, I brushed her hair from her cheek, then froze. Her cheeks were blazing hot, explaining the grogginess.

Hadley always had a weaker immune system, and it seemed to get worse when she was experiencing stress. I could definitely tell that me working more over the last couple of weeks, leaving her with Lacy, was wearing on her immunity. She doesn't sleep well when I leave her with Lacy, and she clearly got so run down. I'd told myself I was imagining it, but like clockwork, here she was, sick.

Sighing heavily, it didn't release any tension as more flowed in. Lacy wouldn't be thrilled to take Hadley for the weekend if she was sick again. I didn't have anyone else to call. "I can't do this parent thing," I spat out, grabbing my phone and scrolling through my contacts. There was no one to call. No one I trusted to watch Hadley. I had known it was going to be hard to raise a child on my own when I accepted this role, but I wished I had considered how important it was to have a whole village.

I didn't have a village.

It was her and me.

If she was sick, she needed *me*.

Maybe it was a growing thing, and she'd be fine in a couple of hours. "Hadley, does your stomach hurt?" She finally opened her mouth, but not to answer me. Instead, she vomited right into my lap. "Lovely." I couldn't even be mad. It was just how life worked out. Or, really, how it didn't work out. *Ever.*

I ran to the kitchen for the trash can and set it next to Hadley, even though she'd already emptied everything on me. Then I jogged to my bedroom, and took off my shirt, dropping it in the hamper as I walked past. I had gotten behind on laundry in the bustle of working extra this week to make money for this trip, and the hamper overflowed. I rushed to my dresser drawer, pulled out an old pair of sweatpants, and changed.

When I returned to Hadley, she was resting again, her cheeks deep red. I grabbed my phone, noting I had about thirty minutes before I risked missing my flight. If it was something she ate, she'd be better in a few hours. *I didn't have time to wait.* There wasn't a later flight if I wanted to make it to the wedding. I opened my text messages and found one waiting for me.

Elinora: I'm going to bed but I wanted to say good-night. I can't wait to see you tomorrow! Best day ever! My whole family is excited to have you here.

My fingers froze midair. I couldn't reply to that. How was I supposed to tell her I couldn't come? *It would crush her.* It was all she'd been talking about for two weeks. I wanted to go. I wanted to be that guy for her. The one who showed up, and who made her family proud. I had emptied out all of my savings and even picked up two extra shifts at the bar last week to afford that plane ticket and the extra expenses.

Nobody wanted to be there for her more than I did.

I squeezed my hands into fist, and they trembled as anger bubbled in my chest.

What was I supposed to do?

I couldn't imagine what her dad would do to me when he found out I'd canceled on her. He already hated me. He knew what a disappointment I was. He was going to make my life miserable, which would make Elinora miserable. I didn't know how to do this. Frustration pumped through my veins, and I texted Lacy.

Hey, Hadley just puked. I know it's a long shot, but could you still take her? I hate to ask but it's really important.

Lacy: I'm so sorry to hear that. If it was only me, I could but I don't want to risk getting my daughter sick. I'm so sorry. I'll gladly take her next weekend if she's better.

Next weekend, the wedding will be over. Sure, I didn't even know the couple getting married, but it was important to Elinora and her family. Next weekend, I didn't have a flight, and it's more than likely too late to cancel this one. I never bought travel insurance, because I didn't want the extra expense. The stress pooled in my forehead, and I suppressed a scream as another text flashed from Lacy.

Lacy: Honestly, she's really not been well for a while. I think it's time to take her to the doctor.

Lacy was right. Hadley had been sick more often than not lately. I needed to take her to the doctor but my chest tightened as I realized it meant I would miss my flight. This wasn't fair. I wasn't doing anything wrong. I wanted to see my girlfriend. Now, she was going to be disappointed.

I couldn't leave my daughter when she was so sick. If I was honest with myself, I'd caused this by letting Hadley stay at Lacy's too much. She needed to be home. All I'd ever wanted for her was a stable home with a parent who was there for her. Something I'd never had, and I wasn't being here for her the way I had promised her I would be. I can't keep leaving...but if I didn't leave her, I couldn't be there for Elinora.

Hadley moaned in her sleep, her sweet cheeks flushed more. I grabbed her blanket, wrapping it around her, and scooped her up, ready to take her to a walk-in clinic. Something wasn't right. I hated this timing because I wanted to be there for Elinora, but Elinora wasn't my four-year-old daughter.

There really wasn't a way I could be there for both. Not when we lived on different ends of the country. I stared at my phone, not texting Elinora back. I couldn't tell her what a disappointment I was. Perhaps it was better she found out now.

As much as I wanted to love her.

Make her my everything.

In my heart, I knew I would always fail her—*like I'd failed myself.*

Man, I didn't have a doubt in the world that I could get on one knee right now and *beg* for her hand in marriage, but I wasn't worthy of that—or her. I'd only mess that up too. The only thing I could do well for her was break her.

A memory popped up. The one when I had overheard Ron telling Elinora that I was going to ruin her. I'd suffered a lot of disappointments in life and few stung worse than that moment, and it always crept up when I was feeling at my worst. It wasn't just what Ron thought, though. It's what everyone thought of me.

I'd heard a lot of people's opinion of me in my life, and this one is always the loudest, ringing over and over in my head. No matter what I'd tried, I can't shut it down.

Maybe it's because Ron was right?

I would ruin her.

It didn't matter that I loved her. It was better to let her go. I wasn't worthy of her, and I was fooling myself to think I could ever make her happy.

Fifteen

ELINORA

Ten Years Later

"Um, just in case anyone finds a corpse in the janitorial closet"—I shifted my eyes from side to side, making sure the boss wasn't listening— "it's mine."

My receptionist, Mabel's, jaw fell so low it practically became unhinged. "I totally saw this episode on True Crime, and it doesn't end well," she hissed. "You need to pack your bags and get to Mexico now."

"It's fine." I rebalanced my coffee on top of my stack of binders, doing my best to keep my computer bag secured on my shoulder. "My dad was here." My books were steady now, and I returned my gaze to Mabel, who sat stiffly behind the real estate office receptionist's desk. Her face was a shade of shock, matching her more-strawberry-than-blonde hair.

"Should we call someone to help him?" she asked, concealing her mouth with a cupped palm.

"Oh!" My eyes rounded. "My dad's not *in* there. What kind of mind do you have?" I flashed my eyes heavenward as this conversation was going in a completely different direction than I had planned. "My dad left me a present for my new office. I'm holding it in the closet while the paint dries in my office."

Mabel tilted her car toward me while scratching it. "Uh—"

"He's the taxidermy guy." I waved my hand dismissively as I forgot she had no idea who my dad was. "I know it's weird. I can't stop it. I've tried, but he loves it. It's how he always provided, and I have learned to accept who he is." I rambled as I didn't have time to waste. My dad's unexpected visit this morning had thrown off my schedule, and I was running late for our planning meeting. That shouldn't be a huge deal, but I was still the newest hire, and under the closest microscope. Although I had recently passed the bar exam, I hadn't been immediately offered a position as a corporate lawyer. Instead, my contract listed me as their "legal clerk." I'd wanted to argue, but I needed a job. I hoped a promotion was coming, and the rumors floating around the office were promising. Still not wanting to wreck my chances, I scurried down the hall to the boardroom.

Our office suite was in the corner of a high-rise building, and all the doors were glass. Even when they were closed, one could see exactly what was going on inside, which wasn't the worst part. The absolute terrible part was everyone could see me walking down the hall, and there was no way I'd be able to casually sneak into the room. I worked in a real-life fishbowl.

I attempted to pad softly down the wood floors, but my new pencil skirt kept riding up my tummy rolls, landing dangerously close to my armpits. It was all I could do to covertly tug it down and not spill my coffee. I was the only woman who had ever fantasized about wearing maternity clothes when I wasn't pregnant. When Mabel had been pregnant, she'd worn pants with all these fantastic elastic bands that conformed to the shape of her bump, and they could stretch for days. *They were my dream pants.* She'd come into work, complaining about her pants, but I couldn't help but wish I could try them. *I wanted conforming elastic.* In what society do we normalize maternity pants, because that's the one where I wanted to live.

Just make it through the meeting without a wardrobe malfunction, and the rest of the day should be a cinch. And not like the unbreathable cinch of my skirt. The good kind.

I flexed my lips, landing in a toothy grin as I opened the glass door, and shimmied slowly against the wall, eyes on the empty leather seat closest to me.

"Elinora." Jonathan Fox, my boss and CEO of the company, pronounced my name as if he was a preschooler still trying to grasp the concept of syllables and handed me a matte black folder. "It's the rubric for your evaluations. Please look it over when you have time."

"Yes, sir." I eyed the folder, wondering how I was supposed to grab it with my hands so full, but he did me a favor and slid it on the table in front of an empty seat. I plopped down onto my chair and managed to drop my stack of binders while only spilling one drop of coffee on the table. I quickly smudged it out with my thumb and licked off the remnants before anyone noticed.

"Now that everyone is here, we will begin." Jonathan went into presentation mode as he flicked on a projector with a PowerPoint slide. "Last week, everyone renewed their work contracts. Many of you expressed concerns about not getting raises. That was an intentional delay due to some developments and the reason why contracts were only renewed for six months. As you know, I've been the sole owner of Platinum Real Estate for over thirty years. This year has proved challenging due to my recent health issues. I've decided to take a step back from the daily management, and I am bringing in a few partners." Jonathan paced to the other side of the room while letting his eyes scan the packed boardroom. "I've delegated this Tampa office to my son. One of his first orders of business is to complete your job evaluations as we restructure, and then we will assign salary recommendations based on the restructuring." He pulled his lips into an excited smile, but when paired with his newly grown mustache, he looked like the Monopoly guy. "We will welcome your new boss, also Mr. Fox, in the office sometime later this week."

I was mostly listening to this excuses-to-why-we-never-got-raises speech, but I was more concerned about my stupid skirt riding up my rib cage again. This skirt clearly had a mind of its own, preferring to travel the northern hemisphere. I'd leave it up there if I had the length to spare, but I needed to pull it down or I'd risk showing someone my nether regions. I crossed my legs for extra protection and shifted in my seat, doing my best to sneak an adjustment just as the glass door behind me opened.

Fresh air wafted in.

All googly eyes aimed my way as I leaned forward, grabbed both sides of my skirt, and yanked it down as if I were digging out a wedgie. My face instantly flamed with embarrassment as I dropped back to my seat, my gaze on my lap.

Crud. Crud. Triple crud.

I was pretty sure whoever was standing behind me had gotten a front row seat to me "adjusting my skirt," and I couldn't bring myself to turn around. My stomach dropped out the bottom, and the heat in the room suddenly amplified to a hundred and forty.

I leaned forward, bracing my forehead with my palm while doing my best to conceal my face by looking down. See? This was why the gator suit had been such a huge asset. Clearly, I wasn't skilled at choosing appropriate office wear. Shopping was a total scam, because clothes always looked so adorbs in all those online ads. The cute pencil skirts with blazers. When you added in a few extra pounds for us plus-size girls those styles became unmanageable.

I fought back a deep cringe so hard my shoulders shook.

The heat on my cheeks grew, and I kept my gaze glued to the table as I felt the human presence behind me walk around the side of the room, meeting Jonathan up front. "Sorry to be late," Mabel squeaked out. "The delivery guy needed some signatures."

It was only Mabel. Still embarrassing but it could have been so much worse. *Phew.*

He paused for a beat while Mabel took the last chair. I steeled my chin down and planted both feet on the floor.

"Yes, as I said before," Jonathan continued, "we'll be setting up individual appointments with each of you starting next month as we continue our restructuring. Any questions?"

I was pretty sure asking my coworkers if they had all seen me pull out a wedgie wasn't appropriate, but it was the only thing that came to mind. I continued to shield my face, and as soon as the meeting adjourned, I gathered my things, and bolted for the door.

Not to brag but I was *smooth.*

Slipping out as if I was invisible, I beelined to the back corner office where I'd be safe hiding behind my stack of real estate contracts all day. I didn't even care that the fresh paint fumes were pungent. It was heaven having my own office after having shared the receptionist desk with Mabel, even if the space had recently been converted from storage and was so far down the corridor that no one came this way. I didn't even exist back here, past the bathrooms and the breakroom, and that's the way I liked it.

As I breezed through the doorway, tension released, and my shoulders fell. I dropped my binders on the floor. Not in a neat pile either as they tumbled over, scattering like a toddler had gotten ahold of them. Then I dropped down into my oversized leather chair, slipped off my shoes, and put my feet on my desk.

The closest thing I'd done to a squat, well, ever. And yes, it wasn't even close.

I grabbed the first binder off the floor, pulled out a contract, and braced it directly in front of my face. Another foreclosure acquisition. I wasn't surprised. It seemed like this real estate firm had swallowed up every foreclosure in South Florida. Sometimes they flipped them, but often we turned them into rental houses, the nicest ones being converted to short-term vacation rentals. My job was to review everything to ensure all the Ts were crossed and no detail was missed.

Townhouses. Six of them. Looked like expensive townhouses, too because the buyout from the bank was over five million dollars. Good ol' Mr. Fox had taken another million out to renovate, citing security upgrades, parking upgrades, and the need to add a community pool. Hmm. It must be nice to have that kind of money.

This was the part of being a lawyer that made me super sleepy. My eyes instantly grew heavy, as I hated paperwork. When I had decided to go back to school for my law degree, I had envisioned myself spending hours arguing in courtrooms, and with my love for talking, that sounded like the best job ever. The caveat I'd never seen coming was I'd LOATHED in all caps my criminal law classes. I had romanticized how cool it would be to argue in court, but when it had come down to helping criminals...I just couldn't. I'd immediately changed my goals.

I wasn't sure it had nothing to do with the fact that I had spent my life being bullied, and I was unable to bring myself to help the jerks.

So, corporate law it was, landing me in real estate only a month ago. I'd admit Jonathan's business had a terrible reputation in this community for being shady, and the position had been open for months as nobody even applied. Still, it was a paycheck, and no one else had offered. My plan was to get some experience and then move on with the next offer. Whenever that was.

Even though I still hadn't been given my official lawyer title, I had started here at six figures, and that would only increase each year. It was a sweet gig, and for the first time in my life, I was getting ahead. Oh, where was I? I forced my gaze back to the contract. Oh yes, so, a second mortgage for renovations, and the inspection was completed—

"What, wait," a voice called from my office door. It teased a familiarity I'd heard before. "Who's in my office?"

I nearly choked as I instantly jolted to my feet like a soldier, yanking on the sides of my northern-bound skirt as my eyes fled to the door. *His office?* I greeted him like I was reporting to a drill sergeant. "Yes, sir!"

Still flustered, my gaze danced around, landing first on his dark suit with iron-creased legs. *Very nice suit.* Possibly Armani. All the way to his hair, longer than I'd expected for an office. Interesting. Borderline rebellious. Finally, my gaze landed on his eyes—set deep behind dark lashes and color just like—

No way!

No, no way.

My feet fumbled back, which set me into an accidental stumble over the chair leg. I barely managed to stabilize myself but kept my eyes on his—*The same color as my mother's ring.* Lightning could have split the room in two, and I still wouldn't have been able to pull my gaze from his.

It had taken me a *full year* to stop crying over him, but the sting in my eyes was as instant as if it was yesterday. A year that I'd never get back for a guy who clearly hadn't cared about me. Not once—but twice that jerk left me heartbroken—both times dropping off the planet. I didn't know if he'd died or got amnesia. Had I been a game? Nobody could have been dirtier than that.

His jaw was steeled. *"Elinora."*

My heart twisted, causing so much constriction. The walls around me literally started to wave.

Graham.

And he had used *my real name*. He never did that. I hated it but sort of loved it, because it always sounded so *hot*. But the bigger issue was, *why was he here?*

"What, who…" My words slowly revved back on. "You don't work—work here, like here." I slammed my palm down on my desk. "Here?" I motioned to him with an accusing finger. "How…how'd that happen? You have a bookstore. In Vermont. Aren't you in Vermont?" I pointed out the window but remembered it looked south. I turned and pointed left, but that was east, so I jerked my hand to the right. "Is that north?"

His lips curled slightly. He was amused. Not mad. That was good. So good. But then again, he was here, and that was bad. So bad. He stepped into the room, and brushed the door closed with his hand. It wasn't all the way closed like an HR scandal waiting to happen. Plus, the door was glass, preventing us from full privacy.

Phew, why was it Mars-hot in here all the sudden?

Had I gone to Mars?

That would explain so much.

Like these hot flashes. I fanned my face with my hand, wishing on all my future birthday candles that this wasn't happening. My heart fluctuated between thumping out, "I love you!" to contracting out, "How could you?" One thing was certain—I was backed up against a wall I had never seen coming.

"Relax." Graham's hand stretched toward me, inviting me to sit back down. I couldn't sit. I had the wrong skirt for sitting. I'd already been over this today. Nope, I was standing with both knees knocking.

"I'm f-fine." A cough bubbled up, as if it was little gas streams from my heart, still piping out the "I love you." Those were clearly betrayals.

His eyes tracked my movements, and he was patient—too patient—as I squirmed at the unbidden feeling of goose-bumps dotting my spine. I wasn't going to beat around the bush. I needed answers. I placed both palms firmly on my desk to steady myself and fixed my gaze on his, my heart twisting in the most heartbreaking way, melting into his gaze. "I'm so confused." His lips turned playful, mischievousness twinkling from beneath his dark lashes. He was clearly enjoying this too much, and I would be lying if I said I hated seeing him again.

Someday, they'll write textbooks about the power of his gaze.

What was wrong with me?

His eyes had somehow gained more power over me, as if they'd taken all the lost years of unrequited love and funneled them into this one glare. I pinched my brow, breaking the pull, and barely stuttered, "G-Graham, what are you doing here?"

Sixteen

GRAHAM

"*Gra*ham." Her eyes bulged from their sockets. Her voice weakened when it floated out with so much emphasis on the second syllable, it was drenched in phlegm and sounded like she growled the word *ham.* It made her sound hungry, and mad, as if she hadn't eaten for days. I wanted to chuckle, because well, that's what Elinora always made me do. No matter how hard I tried to be sober around her, she had a way of being so out of tune that it was impossible to be serious.

But beyond her hangry ham slur, it was her voice. I hadn't heard it in years, but my heart knew it, because it still communicated with her.

Every. Day.

That didn't make me want to smile.

It made my heart bubble up, doing little fizzy pops that somehow simultaneously inoculated me with the flu because now I wanted to vomit. I swallowed my nausea, doing my best to keep a straight face. I sauntered into her office, invading her space. Her face grew ashen, and her lips were agape, but she wasn't talking. "Why do you look so disappointed?"

"That's not disappointment." She yanked on the back of her skirt, adjusting it. "That's just my face."

She was lying. She'd never struggled to talk in her life, and now that her skirt was adjusted, she was frozen. "Are you practicing for a prison photo?"

She blinked, slowly, as if afraid to stir the air too much. "Maybe. It would be better than this."

Ouch.

That was unexpected. I'd admit I had been nervous to see how she reacted to me as her new boss. I'd assumed she'd be shocked, but I had anticipated a warmer welcome than this. Her lips tightened into a straight line, and she stood square with me, planting her feet shoulder width apart. I started to get the impression that my worst fear was true.

She might *not* be happy to see me.

Here was the deal.

My life before, I had been living day to day, hardly making it at first. Lately, though, things have been going sensationally. Yet, I pretended I hadn't made the biggest mistake of my life by pushing her away, but the guy I had been back then would have ruined her.

I hated what I had done to her.

Hated it.

But I would have hated myself more if I had let Hadley down and been the type of parent I'd swore I would never be. When I'd accepted custody of her, I'd swore to God I would make her my first priority, and I didn't take that oath lightly.

It hadn't been a mistake. I replayed the events of years ago all the time. All the memories we had, and even some of the ones we hadn't had time to make together. I couldn't stop imagining in my head. Like how she had looked like a princess, dressed for a wedding in her bridesmaid's gown, her hair and makeup expertly done in the selfie she'd sent while waiting for me to join her. She had been so excited, and I refused to reply. She'd sent another photo later, one with her whole family, and she had sounded optimistic but wondered if my flight had been delayed. The texts had kept coming, sounding more frantic, but I hadn't been able to reply. How could I break her heart? Before I knew it, it was too late, and she had been crying, and I'd finally mustered up all I had to text her.

Graham: I'm sorry, I can't make it. This whole thing isn't going to work out. Just forget about me.

I didn't reply to the dozens of pleas she had sent after that. I couldn't. After many weeks, they'd finally trickled off, and my phone had eventually gone silent. As the years had ticked by, the road had only narrowed into a single path on which all I did was work my butt off to climb the real estate ladder and hang out with Hadley.

But this twist of fate was going to kill me. Actually, it wasn't so much of a twist of fate, because I had known she'd applied for this job. Even though she was grossly under qualified, being a new graduate, I'd championed for her to be hired from behind the curtain. I knew if she understood who worked here, she wouldn't have even stepped foot inside. I made sure she never found out I worked here.

I studied the lines in her face. Those were new. Nothing overly deep, but a few extra smile lines, though she clearly wasn't smiling now. It had been ten years since I'd last seen her, and every remnant of the young Elinora I had known was now gone. Like a fine wine, she had become cultured and radiant.

"I won't accept this." Elinora pointed her finger at me, jabbing it into my chest. "You'd better explain what's going on. Why are you in my office?"

I clasped her hand where it still poked to my chest and dropped it until it swung freely at her side. Clearing my throat, I looked her dead in the eyes. "It's *my* office."

"This is absurd." She threw her hands up in the air and shuffled to the door, her heels clicking the whole way. "I'm going to have Mabel call the cops to escort you out."

"Stop." I caught her hand midair and held it there. "They won't escort me out because it's my building. I'm the new partner."

The look she gave me was indecipherable. She was obviously putting up a mask to prevent me from seeing her true feelings. "You're lying."

"No. Not even a little white lie." I was selfish for delaying the truth. I had never been in this situation or even anything close to it. I had always been the guy who was at the bottom rung of society. Something about the power of those words made my throat burn. This was the reunion I'd always dreamed of. I wasn't vulnerable anymore. I had my life together. I was finally able to win her love forever. "Sit down. I'd love to tell you everything." I glared at her, but she still didn't sit.

Pacing around her, I didn't hold back, "Jonathan Fox is my dad." Her tongue softly clicked behind her parted lips, but she was quiet. "My real dad, whom I never knew."

"Makes sense." Her eyes narrowed. "Both of you are scum."

Ignoring her dig, I went on as if I was recounting a lazy Sunday. "About a decade ago, I saw one of those ancestry commercials on YouTube. A lightning bolt zapped through my brain, demanding me to pay attention. I don't know why I'd never thought of it before. Maybe I was holding onto the hope my mom would eventually have this heart-to-heart with me and tell me who my dad was. As soon as I had the thought, I immediately went online.

When I discovered my dad was Jonathan Fox, owner of one of the most successful real estate firms, I understood why my mom had never told anyone." I raked a hand through my hair, but it quickly cascaded back around my eyes. "He didn't exactly welcome me with open arms, as you can imagine. However, I think the timing was perfect because he had recently been diagnosed with heart disease. I'm pretty sure had I contacted him even a year prior, he would have had nothing to do with me. He was reflecting on things but he didn't want me to tell his wife about me and offered a pile of money and fifty percent partnership in his business. At first, I said no, but it infuriated me to miss out on something that should have been mine and Hadley's right. You saw my life with Hadley before. We were drowning. It didn't take me long to accept a position in his Portland office, and I've worked my tail off every day for nearly a decade to help build this company into what it is. It's paid off. Now, I'm rich, and can afford anything I want for Hadley or myself."

"So." Elinora pressed the tips of her fingers on her lips, as if she was teasing biting a nail. "Is he Hadley's dad too?"

I shook my head, not wanting to entertain any thoughts of another dad for Hadley. *I was her dad.* Always had been. Always would be.

"Okay, now that I understand you are working here..." Her hand snaked around the back of her neck, and she hooked it there, pausing for a beat before saying, "I need to quit. Now." She stood up straighter, pulled her shoulders back, and walked back toward the door.

"That's a breach of contract." Each word I spoke held the sole purpose of getting her to see I'd changed. I was successful now and finally in charge of my life.

"I'm the one who drew up the contract."

"Then you know it's solid." I snatched her hand, feeling the betrayal of my heart skipping a beat. It only ever did that for her. Swallowing to steady the adrenaline, I added, "There's no getting out of it."

"I signed it before I knew who I was working for." She tried to shake off my hand, but I held onto it as if she was already mine again. "I think we both understand that it's not a good work environment for us to work together. *You* can do the right thing, and we can come to a mutual understanding that the contract was misrepresented." She took a wide step away, forcing me to drop her hand.

I shook my head. I couldn't do that. She would walk out of this door and never talk to me again. Every nerve in my body tensed as I understood this was my one shot to finally make Elinora mine forever. I wasn't a fool. I had blown it. I should have fought harder last time, but I wouldn't repeat my mistake again. I was playing for keeps this time. "Relax, it's just six months." I sauntered over to her desk and sat on the chair, putting my feet on her desk. "Perhaps, we can share the office. You won't even notice I'm here."

Seventeen

Elinora

"I need some air." That was the only audible thing I could muster as I finally pushed past him and out the door. Inside I was still screaming *I hate you alongside I love you,* but I also added, *What happened to you?*

Never in my wildest dreams had I thought I'd ever run into Graham again, especially when he had suddenly become the guy I depend on for my livelihood. It was beyond cruel. I needed my job. With student loans lighting up my phone notifications several times a month, I was not in a position to breach my work contract. I would lose my income while scarring my work history.

But I couldn't see him every day!

Just being near him made my blood pressure soar. I wasn't emotionally immature. I could separate work from personal life. My mind was logical. I could ignore him. Shoot, I usually just hid in paperwork all day. But nothing about this was logical! It was pure emotion. My heart was misbehaving, reminding me of all the nights I had thought of Graham. This was never going to work. I'd rather be homeless than work next to him.

Would I? Okay, being homeless might be a bit of a stretch.

I reached the lobby and took a lap around the waiting area. When that didn't help to calm me down, I looped around again like I was stuck in a cul-de-sac. Mabel rose from her desk, observing me like her favorite hamster on a workout wheel. "Perhaps you could do that outside around the block?" She jerked her head toward the boardroom, the one with glass walls. The finance team was having a meeting, and although they were used to my oddities, the bankers accompanying them weren't. "We don't need to look like a bunch of crazies with our payroll on the line."

"It's not on the line," I huffed out, planting my feet in the middle of the room, speaking too sharply.

"Rumor is," Mabel covered her mouth with her palm while leaning closer, "Jonathan sent his son here for a reason."

"Yeah," I bite back quickly, "to bleed my heart dry."

"Well, he is cute, but that's not why he's here. He's here to close the office. That's why we didn't get raises."

"That makes no sense." I stopped pacing and raised my hands to my head, balancing them on top of it, as if I was ready to start some awkward Richard Simmons' stretches. I didn't have a clue what to do with myself. My heart revolted against my years of unrequited love but I couldn't forget my financial need. "We just renewed our contracts."

"For six months." She tilted her head toward me. "Who offers only a six-month contract with no raises?"

"Scum like Jonathan Fox." I didn't even flinch, as that made sense. Or did it? "I need fresh air," I blurted out as I spun on my heel and bolted out the door, knowing I wasn't coming back to the office today. I didn't care if I got fired. That would be a break from my contract, which was exactly what I needed. I had finally gotten my life together with this job. It wasn't perfect but it was the most money I'd ever made, and it was building my resume. Once again, Graham was ruining my life.

Eighteen

GRAHAM

The following morning, I sat in our shared office, waiting for Elinora to arrive at work. Unable to concentrate, my gaze kept sliding to the empty doorway. When she hadn't arrived by ten, I knew the game she was playing. She was never tardy. She was the gal who was always ten minutes early, if not twenty, and then would proceed to drive around the block five times, trying not to look too eager. I picked up my phone and texted her.

Me: You are late for work.

Elinora: I quit.

Me: Sorry, but you can't. I'm on my way out for an early lunch. I'll pick you up.

Elinora: Drop dead.

Me: Excited to work with you, too.

Stuffing my phone in my pocket, I cleared the files from my desk and briskly walked out the door. This was a long shot—winning her back. I knew I didn't deserve another chance. But, if I couldn't have her love, I didn't want anyone else's. I wasn't going to let her become my Farewell to Arms.

Once in the parking garage, I walked over to my Maserati and got in, fully remembering that the last time I'd picked her up, I had been driving my old Toyota. It was mind blowing how when I'd had nothing, she had looked at me as if I was everything. I remembered scraping change out of the middle console of my car to be able to buy her a Cherry Coke. Now that I have everything, she glared at me like I was nothing.

I would change her mind.

I punched in the address I'd stolen from her employee file into my GPS and pulled out of my parking spot without even a question about how crazy this made me look. I wasn't acting out of desperation. I honestly lacked nothing in my life. I'd never had a lack of options for female companionship. I'd always pushed for the unattainable. If it was easy, something everyone could have, I didn't want it. That included women. I never give up on anything I wanted. I pushed hard. Perhaps too hard. What was the point of that desire if you weren't willing to fight for it?

Elinora.

Elinora was more than something to chase.

She was everything worth fighting for.

As much as I'd tried to forget her, I couldn't erase her from my soul. Our souls had been stitched together years ago. My heart thumped rapidly against my chest as I sped to her house. This could very well be the last chance I had. If I didn't change her mind during these short six months, I doubted I would ever see her again.

I needed her to see how everything in my life was wrong without her. We belonged together. I was finally in a position to give her the life she deserved with everything she'd ever wanted—even more than she'd ever dreamed of. All the love she'd ever desired. We could do anything. Go anywhere. Anything her heart could fathom, and I wouldn't have a preference, because all I wanted was to do life with her. I'd seen the flickers in her eyes. She still loved me. And I needed to get her to trust me again.

I pulled up in front of the house my GPS had guided me to and texted her.

Me: Outside.

Elinora: Get lost.

Me: Ah, thanks for the invite. Don't mind if I do come in.

Elinora: You're not invited in.

Me: You're on my time.

Elinora: Whatever. I'll come out, but ONLY so we can settle this.

Tapping my fingers on the steering wheel, I waited for a minute before she strode out her front door. Her shoulders were back, her hair flowing down in the soft wind, and she wore an all-business expression on her face. With her laptop bag slung over her shoulder and her business-appropriate attire, she certainly appeared ready for work. She opened the door without looking at me, slid in, and buckled. "You're a jerk," she muttered, staring forward.

"You have a contract, and without a medical exemption, legal obligation, incarceration, or death, you're bound to that contract."

"After all these years, I finally understand how desperate you were to vandalize public property. I'd do anything to go to jail right now."

"We've always had so many things in common," I teased with a humored inflection, my heart still knocking hard on my chest. I was desperate to wipe the scowl from her face, missing so terribly the days when she'd turn to me and willingly kiss me. I rolled my bottom lip in and bit back the taste I swore still lingered. It had been ten years since I'd kissed her. I didn't care if it took me the next ten years to get her to kiss me again. It would be worth it. I pulled forward and softened my voice. "Are you hungry?"

She tsked but didn't look my way.

"Well, I'm starving." I pulled out into traffic and steered toward the office. "How about sushi before we go back?"

Without flinching, she spat out, "Sorry, I cut everything parasitic from my life."

"Ouch." I gripped the steering wheel harder, inhaling a breath that sliced through my clenched teeth. In my twenties, I'd been passive-aggressive about some things, but I'd learned a thing or two about going after what I wanted. I wasn't about to waste my time waffling around. "We need to talk about some stuff."

"You said you were taking me to work, not discussing the past. Now you're a liar, too." She crossed her arms over her body, shifting in her seat, angling her body even farther away from me. "You've finally gotten what you wanted after all these years. I'm keeping my mouth shut."

Nearly veering off the road, I yanked the wheel and stopped on the shoulder, resisting the urge to pound my fist on the dash. Nobody hated me more than I did for what I had done, but getting angry wasn't going to solve anything. "I hope it's not too late to say I'm sorry."

"Don't give me any of that boy band lyric bologna." She shuffled her feet before spouting off, "Can you please drive this car? Otherwise, I'm going to walk. I have no interest in sitting in here with you."

I pushed my tongue to the roof of my mouth, halting my words. Bickering wasn't going to help. She needed to know how messed up things were. "Look, I screwed up. In my head, I have taken it back a thousand times over, but that doesn't translate to reality. We have to get past this. What do you need from me?"

"I need you to let me out of my contract and leave me alone."

"I can't do that." My voice cracked, slayed at the mere thought of never seeing her again.

"Look." She angled her head slightly, but still didn't meet my gaze. "You want me to talk. I'll talk. I can't do this. You think you can swoop in here as my boss and impress me, but it doesn't. I'm not shallow. I don't care if you have money now. I can't even sit next to you. That's why I couldn't come into the office. You want to be a jerk and hammer in that last nail in our relationship coffin, so that I hate you even more, then make me stay in this contract. Fine. I'll finish the contract, but I can't see you every day. You can have my office. I'll work in the janitor's closet if that means I won't have to look at you."

"You're right. Sorry isn't what you need to hear." I raked my hands through my hair, the heat nearly boiling from my scalp. Before I knew what I was doing, I grabbed her hand. It trembled in mine as I pulled it close to me. "I wanted you, but I was bad for you. As much as you hate me now, you would have hated me more if I'd dragged you through the last ten years. I promise you I would have broken you so many times more if I had carried you through the trauma from which I emerged. I promise you now, things are different."

"What trauma are you even talking about? So you had a hard life. I'm sorry, that doesn't give you a free ticket to treat someone like a jerk!"

"I was nothing," I blurted out. "I was a total loser, stuck in poverty and in survival mode, just trying to keep Hadley alive and a leaky roof over our head. Hadley got super sick the night I was supposed to leave on the plane to see you. I panicked thinking I was failing her, and it was my fault she was sick. I needed to make sure I was putting her first." I shook my head, refusing to go back to those years, even if it was just a memory.

"Do you really think I wouldn't have understood about Hadley? I understood she needed you. I was willing to meet you where you were, and I would have loved Hadley too." Her eyelashes fluttered as if she'd absorbed a bullet to the heart, and she yanked back her hand. "Your words are poison."

"Get it out," I urged, hating how her lips twisted into a menacing scowl. We'd never get past our issues if she didn't let out her hurt, but I also knew this wasn't her real self. The real Elinora—*the one who's heart I knew*—had more empathy than this. She had a shield up. A shield that I triggered, as a reaction to her heartbreak. Something I knew a lot about, but I also know we had to talk about it to get over it. "I agree with you. I did everything wrong."

"You ghosted me." Tears layered in her eyes, and although her words were seeped in spite, the crack in her voice told me her anger was merely another shield of protection. "I quit my job to move across the country for you and you ghosted me!"

"You quit your job?" A perplexed brow sprang up, as I had no idea. Apparently, she suffered more loss than I'd thought. "You never told me that."

"I was willing to give up my whole life for you. I told my whole family about what an amazing guy you were, and you showed me that your words were trash." She sucked in a loud breath as she violently wagged her head back and forth. "I never want to feel that vulnerable again."

"I had no idea you did that." Taking a hard swallow to conceal the crack in my voice, I pushed past the tightening in my chest. It was my fault. Even if she'd tried to tell me, I deleted her texts. I had no idea I'd messed up her life that badly. "My life was such a disaster back then. I didn't want to ruin you too."

"Well, joke's on you. After I finally got done crying, I funneled all the spite you left me with into law school, and I graduated at the top of my class. At least you were good for something."

"I would have never asked you to quit your job. I wasn't worth that," my voice deepened. "I can understand why you're upset. I just hope you understand my intention was to protect you. It killed me to break up with you, but I had to do something drastic because I wanted you to hate me so you could move on. I know it was messed up, but I clearly panicked."

"It worked, because I did move on." She flipped her hair over her shoulder, and jutted her chin, still facing forward, hardened scowl on her face. "I'm never going to believe a thing you say to me ever again."

Swallowing, I gave up on this conversation. *For now.* She was upset but this back-and-forth stuff wasn't us. Though, it was progress—a step toward healing. My heart believed she'd get there, but I had to do the work first. I wasn't quitting. "Okay, sushi it is."

Nineteen

ELINORA

My stomach was a loopy roller coaster whenever I was in the same building as Graham. I paced the lobby, waiting for him to go to his meeting in the boardroom. I couldn't step foot in my office, because Graham had taken over, even moving in another desk so we could be buddies like a couple of grade school kids. I had my laptop, as I never went anywhere without it since I have no life outside of work, but I needed to get my contract binders.

"You look terrified." Mabel spoke to me with her lips attached to the straw that connected to her giant forty-ounce stainless steel mug of water. "Did something happen?"

"Everything happened." I lapped around again, stealing a look down the hall as my office door opened. Ducking behind the corner, I waited for Graham to cross the hall to the boardroom before I let out a giant sigh. I tiptoed until my feet met the front of Mabel's desk and whispered, "You've worked here a long time, right?"

"Four years." She slurped on her straw, which cackled so loudly I winced and checked the hall to ensure we didn't draw anyone's attention. "Have you ever seen Graham—I mean, Mr. Fox—in the office before? I've only been here a month, and this is the first I've heard about him."

"No. His name came across my desk a few times, but he's never been here." Her lips curled at the tips, but they stayed smashed together as if she was trying to hold in top-secret information, before leaking out, "He's pretty nice to look at, isn't he?"

"Sure." I didn't want her to suspect I knew anything more about Graham than she did. I surely didn't want her to know we'd dated. I wished so hard I could be repulsed by the mere suggestion he was good looking, but I couldn't. I'd always been drawn to him, and as much as I hated it, after everything he'd done to me, my eyes magnetically shifted down the hall to the transparent boardroom walls.

Graham sat at the head of the boardroom table; his chair angled a little sideways. One arm was on the table, presenting the sleeve of his suit jacket. Relaxed in his chair, he had one leg crossed at the ankle over the other as he leaned back. He wore an arrogance I'd never seen on him before. Whatever had happened to him these last ten years had changed him, made him different. Cocky. I didn't like it. He never used to be like that. His lack of arrogance had been the thing that had drawn me to him.

"I'm going to work out here today. The light feels better." I cleared my throat as I broke my gaze from Graham before I got caught staring at him. After all, glass walls were transparent in two directions. I took steps down the hall, calling back. "I'm going to grab my stuff—" I froze in the doorway, jaw dropped.

A mason jar of dandelions sat on my desk.

They were mangled, and half wilted, way beyond anything you could pass for rustic chic, but it was the exact thing that melted my heart. Graham knew me. I wasn't into grand gestures or anything expensive. It was the little things that spoke to my heart. The backs of my eyes pricked with tears.

This couldn't happen.

He was pretending nothing had happened. It's like he was trying to pick up where we'd left off. He couldn't do that because he was leaving out the chapter when he'd ghosted me. This would never work.

We weren't friends.

We definitely weren't going to be friends with any benefits.

I strolled to my desk, grabbed the vase, and was about to empty it on his chair but paused. If I did that, he'd know it had affected me. That would only encourage him. I knew how he was. He wouldn't give up on anything until he took it too far.

That included the way he'd dumped me. Fingers trembling, I replaced the weeds on my desk.

"I seized those days." Graham's gravelly voice wafted from behind me, startling me to full attention, and I almost knocked the jar over.

The way Graham always teased a little poetry was a bullet to my heart. Swallowing, I kept my chin down as I fumbled for my notebook and favorite fountain pen. "You seized the wrong days."

He moved to the front of my desk, but I didn't look up, even when his scent wafted under my nose, making my knees buckle, a muted amber musk I'd never smelled on him before that blended well with his natural fragrance. Just another thing about him that had changed. "I seized all my yesterdays with you."

"Shows, because you're clearly stuck in the past." I side-stepped, taking the long way back to the exit in obvious avoidance of him.

"My meeting's over." His feet stayed planted in front of my desk, as if he thought I cared to talk to him.

"I'm working next to Mabel today," I muttered.

"That's fine." In my periphery, I could see him rub his chin. "Can you complete what needs to be done in the office today? Tomorrow, I need you to come with me to close on some condos in Naples."

"That's Finance's job," I asserted as sternly as I could. "You don't need legal at an acquisition closing."

"I didn't ask."

I fought the urge to huff because I knew the game he was playing. I couldn't show him that he was getting to me. "Time?"

"I'd like to leave early. Seven at the latest. I can pick you up on the way out of town."

"I'll be here at six forty-five." I envisioned one of those swinging doors closing behind me as I paced down the hall, but unfortunately, there was no barrier between us, and I could feel his eyes on me the whole way.

I had to find a way out of this contract. My cheeks raged with heat. I'd rather scrub toilets than do this. I dropped my notes on the corner of Mabel's receptionist desk, where I had worked before getting my own office. A sarcastic chuckle bleeped out of my lips. So much for getting my own office. I didn't even have to force a pleading expression. The tension had already boiled past my neck. "I'm having a hard time focusing back there."

"Ah, you miss me." Mabel's face was laced with a giant smile as she pushed her bowl of complimentary mints toward me and winked. "Happy to have you back. Have a treat."

"Thanks." I stuffed my hand in the jar, and pulled out a hard peppermint, squeezing it from the wrapper until it plopped into my mouth. I slumped onto my chair. After setting up my laptop, I pulled up my employment contract and zoomed in. Now, to find the loophole. The only thing I remembered adding required employees to pay back two months' salary to recoup training expenses. I didn't have that much money. But taking out a loan might be worth it. Scouring the contract terms, I'd never wished for a typo more. Something to show this nightmare could end. Oddly, my gaze lowered to the keyboard.

The escape key!

That was what I needed.

I violently pressed it, ringing it over and over, but I stayed put.

My escape key was broken.

Twenty

GRAHAM

It was a sunny fall morning, and I had been awake since 3:30 A.M., thinking about Elinora. She'd seemed to put on a good façade, acting like she was enraged to see me, but the way her gaze had angled to me when she hadn't thought I was looking revealed how I was affecting her. She felt this magnetic pull, too. I was confident she still felt the chemistry. If I could only get her to trust me, she'd know that everything I'd done in the last decade was for us to have a better life.

In hindsight, I should have been honest right away, and maybe kept her in the loop, tried to be friends. My heart knew she wouldn't have let me go through that alone, and I just didn't want to drag her through the years of poverty and single parenthood. My fight-and-flight response had been triggered when Hadley got sick, and I couldn't fathom that she'd ever forgive me for missing the wedding. I hadn't been thinking and I fled. Looking back, I understood it. I had always been in fight or flight mode, and it had taken years of therapy to climb out.

Now, I just want Elinora to look at me the way she used to.

When the clock finally read 5:30, I decided to get in my run. I had taken up running when I was at the boys' ranch as a way to manage my rage, but now I did it to keep my body lithe. What I wouldn't do for my seventeen-year-old metabolism, when the pounds had never even appeared. A clean diet, regular moving and weights kept my body leaner than most people who are in their middle thirties.

Thirty. That was a grave number. I used to think of thirty-year-olds and cringe, believing all their fun was behind them, but I had just gotten my life together. Once I win Elinora's loyalty back, our lives together would just be starting.

I ran my three miles, timing myself the whole way. I made it in an even twenty-three minutes. Most people run to up tempo beats, but I used this time for my audio books. Today's listen? The Hobbit. I'd read the book at least a dozen times, but this was the first time I'd heard a voice performance. I hated to turn it off when I reached for my phone at the end of my run.

I swiped away my audiobook, revealing the photo I had of Elinora and me as my screensaver. I had taken it on our first—and last—date. We'd been lying under the stars for an hour already, and I reached up and snapped an aerial-view selfie. It was funny how I'd thought I would have more time to get photos and document our relationship, but everything had imploded after that trip. This was the only thing I had from that whirlwind. That, and the memories pounding in my chest that echoed whenever I thought about how it had felt to kiss her.

There I was again.

I jogged right up to the garage entrance of the mansion, officially owned by my sperm donor, Jonathan Fox. The pad had been another hush present. But for me, it was a place to stay while I hunted for something better. I rushed up the stairs, hoping to beat Hadley before she locked herself in the bathroom. Not that I need to fight her for the bathroom. We had five of them. She was at that stage when once she went into the bathroom, it was impossible to talk to her.

Teenage girls were an enigma.

I wasn't sure what had happened to the little girl she had been, but now when I looked at her, all I saw was someone who was annoyed about my entire existence. I passed through the front door. One look down the hall revealed her bedroom door wide open. I didn't even need to turn my head the other way to know the bathroom was locked up tighter than Fort Knox. "Hey, Hads," I hollered through the door. "I'll start breakfast. Do you want eggs or French toast?"

"Neither."

"You gotta eat something. Lunch is six hours from now." Shifting my weight on my legs back and forth, I struggled to maintain my patience. I missed the days when she allowed me to make decisions for her. Everything felt like a bargaining game these days. "How about a smoothie? I bought some of that weird vegan rice milk you like."

"Do we have any bananas?"

I rubbed my temples, struggling to maintain an even tone. "Frozen, but they should blend."

"Can you add chocolate?"

"For breakfast?"

"*Dad*," she hollered as if I'd forgotten who I was in this conversation.

"Hads."

"It'll be fine."

"How much longer do you need in there?" I stared at the door, visualizing all the bottles of toiletries she'd amassed spread out over the entire bathroom counter. She was into this new skincare line she had seen on TikTok. Each bottle was like sixty bucks. It seemed absurd to me to pay that much for this stuff, but I let her get whatever she wanted because I could finally afford to spoil her. "I was hoping I could see your face this year."

"Twenty more minutes."

I flashed a look heavenward, as there was no way I could spend more than twenty minutes total getting ready. "I'll make us a couple of smoothies. They'll be ready when you're done."

Silence.

Not I-didn't-hear-you silence, but the silence that was teenage code for parents are annoying. I got it. I'd gone through that phase too. Sometimes I thought I was still partially in it.

I sauntered down the hall, scrolling through the morning news on my phone. I wasn't a huge news junkie—as none of the stuff that was public was ever good news. I allowed a solid five minutes of the morning headlines before forcing myself to think about positive things. It was another trick I'd learned in therapy. I'd spent so much time in therapy, you'd think I could be a therapist by now. It didn't work like that, though.

I gathered ingredients for smoothies, blending everything together as I had done many times while working at the bookstore. Part of me would always miss that place. I'd never dreamed of working for a real estate giant, but the money was better. Partnering with my bio dad had gotten us out of poverty, and Hadley gained access to the best private school. For the first time ever, I felt like life wasn't totally ruining her.

I still missed that bookstore.

Since I had become rich, I'd kept the little store and now paid a guy named Joe to run it. It didn't make any profit, but I don't care. It was a hobby I couldn't let go. While I poured the smoothies into cups, Hadley padded into the kitchen. "I forgot I have drama practice before school. We're going to run lines, and I need to go in early."

I handed her cup over, scanning her outfit, another thing I'd learned too late I needed to do daily. It wasn't until I had gotten a call from the school about her halter top that I'd figured out she was going to fight me about this. Again, I'd gone through the defiance phase, and I understood it. This was some cosmic payback. She was wearing high-waisted jeans, and a dark flannel shirt with a tank underneath. "Can you button your shirt?"

"Dad."

"It must have shrunken in the wash, or maybe you grew. It doesn't fit well."

"It's supposed to fit like this."

"Button your shirt."

"You know I'm going to unbutton it when I get to school," she huffed as her fingers found the bottom button.

"At least I won't have to lie when the school calls me, accusing me of letting you come to school in a halter top. I can tell them that when I dropped you off, you were wearing a buttoned flannel."

"You're buggin'." She rolled her eyes, but she continued to button her shirt as she moved to the door and grabbed her backpack.

"What are you doing?" I moved to the sink to rinse out the blender. "Have a seat. I still need to shower."

"Dad, I have drama practice."

"Hads," I echoed the edge in her voice. "You always have *drama*."

"We gotta go now." She headed toward the door, twisting the knob.

I wanted to scream out in annoyance. It should be illegal for people to parent teens without some special certification, which I was clearly lacking. I took a minute to wipe off the counter and checked the clock. She was right. If she wasn't going to be late, we needed to leave, which meant I needed to change in under a minute. No shower for me. Now my goal was to slather on so much deodorant it would make me smell like a deodorant factory.

This was my crazy life.

I could hire a driver to do this every day, but I had vowed I'd be the dad who was *actually there* for his child, and that meant every day I did school drop-off and pick-up. "Okay," I muttered as I scrimmaged down the hall, calling back. "Go ahead and get in the car. I'll be down in two minutes."

Twenty-One

ELINORA

Outside the office, I shoved red licorice in my mouth as I paced the parking garage, waiting for Graham's car. He was officially ten minutes late. Not that I'd never been late before. That was not the point. He was trying to find ways to annoy me on top of me hating him.

It was working.

I had been awake most of the night and decided the best way out of this contract was a new approach. Instead of being angry and fighting him, I was going to pretend he didn't bother me at all. Once he realized he couldn't affect me, he'd stop trying so hard and perhaps get bored. It was worth a shot.

His car rolled slowly through the narrow pass and stopped beside me. Swallowing my frustrations while plastering a pleasant smile on my face, I opened the door and greeted him cheerfully. "Good morning."

With a suspicious side-eye, he watched me buckle in before echoing my greeting. "Good morning."

I didn't mention anything about him being late, or the fact that his cologne, or whatever he was obviously wearing to impress me, was so pungent, it burned my nose. "How are you?"

"I'm okay." His eyes washed over my body as if he was searching for clues about something wrong with me before putting the car into gear and driving forward. "Do you need to stop for anything on the way out of town? A Cherry Coke?"

"Nope." I pulled another strand of licorice from the small package I had stuffed in my coat pocket and purposely didn't offer him one while I proceeded to chew it with my mouth open, smacking as loudly as I could. "Gorgeous morning out, isn't it?" I said with half a stick of licorice in my mouth. If he insisted on spending time with me, I was going to make this as unpleasant for him as possible.

"Yeah, I love Florida mornings."

"Before I forget..." I swallowed my candy, as I had something important to bring up. "I, ah, was going over some of the loan closing papers you conveniently left on my desk last night promptly at five, and there's an error in the price agreement."

"There's never an error in price. The finance team is seamless."

"I can show you." I snaked a hand into the work bag tucked by my foot, and I removed the first stack of papers. "The purchase agreement on this condo, 4A at 1298 Duplin Avenue, is for 978K. I cross referenced that with the loan papers for 1.2M with some notes about taking additional funds for upgrades to the kitchen, fence, and adding new concrete to the driveway. I went back through the estimates for all those things. The loan is still at least a hundred thousand too much, if not way more. It's not making sense why you need all that money, or even why the bank would allow you to take that out. The loan exceeded the property estimate, even with the improvements added in. It could be a typo on the part of the bank, unless you have a plan for those funds that isn't outlined in the improvements?"

"That purchase agreement was made by Jonathan, and he's been doing this for decades. I doubt there's a mistake. I'm sure you're missing something."

"I read all these contracts three times last night, and I can assure you, unless there's a typo, I'm not missing anything. Something is up with your bougie dad."

"Three times?" A smile budded on his lips as he merged onto the freeway, keeping his gaze locked forward. "Sounds like you have an exciting life."

"I had a very enjoyable evening." Biting my tongue, I counted to ten. There was no way I was going to let him get to me. I lowered my gaze to the papers on my lap, pretending to read them again. I wasn't wrong about this. It was clear in the documentation. The more I thought about what could really be happening, and added to what I already suspected about Jonathan Fox, I was starting to think Jonathan was running a scam. One where he took out extra loan money to fund his extravagant lifestyle. I shifted my feet, trying to get comfortable even though I had ample leg room. It was the tension in the air that's making my anxiety pique.

As much as I hated Graham, some small part of me didn't want to see him get wrapped up in his father's illegal shenanigans. He'd had enough bad things happen to him that weren't his fault. He clearly had some rose-colored glasses on about who his dad really was, and I knew it would be pointless to try to convince him otherwise.

We hardly spoke as he drove to the airport and we boarded a small private jet, which took us right to Naples and the private car waiting for us. When we finally pulled into the condo complex, I did a double take. I wouldn't call it a ghetto by any means, but even in this zip code, there was no way these outdated condos would sell for a million each. On the end of a dead-end street, the building butted up against an industrial complex. Each unit desperately needed paint, landscaping, and a good old-fashioned scrub. With the weeds nearly waist high, they appeared abandoned. "Are you sure this is the right place?" I riffled through my papers again, checking the address. "Maybe there are two Duplin Streets, and we're on the wrong one?"

"This is the address. I'll admit it's not what I expected from the listing summary." He parked in the driveway and killed the engine. "We're going to do a fast walk through, and then head to the bank."

"Do we need hazmat suits?" I opened the car door and hopped out, warily eyeing the industrial complex next door. I couldn't tell what they were building, but it was noisy, not at all an inviting residential area. I refused to crack a smile as we paced to the front door together. We were not surprised when the door wasn't even locked, and we pushed it wide open with no key.

"Something tells me this isn't good." Ominous vibes trickled up my spine. I didn't doubt the single hair on my chin would be standing straight out if I hadn't diligently plucked it off this morning just as I had done every morning since turning thirty-five.

"Ah, it's probably some neighborhood kids messing around." Although he seemed to brush off the vandalism, he slowly strode forward. We entered the kitchen, a dingy eggshell-colored room missing all its appliances. The once white cabinets were mucked up with so much dirt, there was no way you could even clean them without straight bleach. A roach family of four crawled in an almost-perfect line on the floor. I shuddered.

"No wonder they took out money for a kitchen remodel. I wouldn't make mud pies here." I stuffed my hands in my pant pockets to minimize the risk of accidentally touching something.

"It didn't say how long this place sat empty. Sometimes dust accumulates."

"Dust?" I snorted, checking the clearing above my head as we passed through the door to the hall. There was no way I was getting caught in a spider web.

"From the summary, the kitchen is the worst of this place. The rest shouldn't be so bad—" His voice dropped off as we both saw the living room at the same time. Other than a single couch against the wall, the wood floor was covered with literal trash, empty bottles and soured milk containers. My hand fled to my mouth as I identified the sight—and smell—of dirty diapers. The large window was cracked, and it must have leaked when it rained, as evidenced by the puddle of water on the floor. And the crowning feature—a massive mold culture was growing in and around the leak.

"I'm out of here." I backed into the kitchen, not needing to see any more of the house. "I don't think it's safe to be here without a mask," I hollered as Graham took another minute to look inside both bedrooms down the hall.

His lips were sealed tight when he circled back. "I've seen enough."

"I can't get over the purchase price of this unit." I was relieved we were leaving. "You'd have to pay me to take this out of your hands. I wonder if Jonathan plans to tear down these condos to have them rezoned. Maybe that industrial complex next door wanted to buy them. It doesn't make sense."

"Haven't you figured out by now that nothing in my life makes sense?" His glare was stone cold, tipping me off that he now believed as I did—that Jonathan was running some sort of scam.

"What are we going to do?" I climbed back in the car and buckled in, relieved to close my car door, adding a barrier between this place and me. "I can't go to that loan closing and pretend everything's okay. It doesn't make sense that the bank would even issue this loan. How did the assessment come in at a million dollars? I know this is Naples, but mold in the middle of the living room? You can bet there's more damage you can't see."

"Unless they are all in on it." Graham stared out the windshield, studying the property.

"Who's all in on it?"

"Everyone. His banker buddies. The appraiser. They must all be taking their cut."

"I can't believe nobody has caught on to this before."

"He usually doesn't let anyone from the Tampa office see anything other than the papers and legal work. He scouts the properties himself. Had his health been better, he would have been here."

"Yeah, but he has to know you won't put up with this."

"Does he?" Graham's expression froze. "Maybe he's testing me? He did offer me a cut of the deal. I didn't know it was shady at the time. I thought he had found a foreclosure that was undervalued."

"You know…" I twisted in my seat, pulling out my laptop from the bag where I had stuffed it in the backseat. "Let me look at something. I've been reviewing these contracts for weeks. Whenever he agrees to purchase something, there's always extra loan money to improve it. I never saw any of the conditions before, but nothing adds up that the bank would allow a million-dollar loan on that petri dish." I opened the first set of documents, scrolling to show Graham. Neither of us spoke as I flipped through the files. Every single one had a second mortgage attached to the principal mortgage. "I picked up on this right away, but I assumed he was buying fixer-uppers that were actually fixable. How long have you worked for Jonathan?"

"Almost ten years." He started the car, backed out of the drive, and we fell into silence as we drove back the way we'd come.

"Are we going to the bank?" After a few minutes of traveling, and I had gathered we were headed back to the interstate toward the airport.

"I'll say something came up."

"Do you think he's setting you up?"

"How do you mean?"

"Does he want you to take the fall for it? Do you think it's a little weird he welcomed you into his life and gave you half of his company with no experience? Not to insult you, but what do you even know about real estate?"

"I didn't know anything at first, but I spent years with him in his Portland office. I've worked my way up. I've done my time." Pausing, he turned to check his blind spot while he merged back onto the interstate. His lips were tightly pressed together. With the traffic heavier than normal, I sank back in my seat and remained quiet.

It was clear to me that this whole deal was a scam, and it had to be clear to Graham. Was Graham in on it? It was illegal, and he'd go to jail if he got caught. *I could go to jail.* Suddenly, the iron-clad employment contracts and lifetime non-disclosure agreements made so much sense. I swallowed, my palms dampened from sweat pulsing out my pores. How was I going to get out of this? Jonathan was a bad dude.

Would he kill me if he knew I knew?

Twenty-Two

GRAHAM

We landed back in Tampa, got back in my car, and Elinora was quiet when I missed the exit to the office. She understood we couldn't go back there yet. I drove toward the bay, finding an Irish pub, and took an upfront parking spot. "Let's...uh, let's get some food."

We got out of the car at the same time, but I stepped behind her, allowing her to pick a table, and we sullenly slid into our seats. The waitress came over, wearing a low braided ponytail down the center of her back and a t-shirt with a logo on it. "Hey, guys! We have a breaded tilapia special today. It comes with fries and coleslaw."

I shrugged, not caring to look at a menu. "Cheeseburger is fine."

"Same." Elinora echoed, and she scooted farther into the booth. "And water, please."

"For me too, please," I added.

As soon as the waitress disappeared, Elinora leaned in, "Is now a good time to insist you let me out of my contract?"

My brows beaded together as confusion about how she could even think about that clouded my mind. "That's still your main focus?"

"Well, yeah. I'm sorry if it's easy for you, but I can't work with you, and I definitely don't want to be part of any illegal scam. I can make a big deal about it, threatening to expose Jonathan, or you can shred the contract. I won't say anything."

"I wasn't even supposed to scout that property, and actually—"

"Actually, what?" That sounded like a challenge.

My mind bounced from the sudden change of conversation as anger bubbled in my chest. "Jonathan told me to leave those acquisitions to the finance team. He seemed very stern about not needing me out in the field—"

She leaned forward with her palms on the table. "That feels like proof he's doing something illegal, and his guys are in on it."

I chewed the inside of my cheek. There wasn't any other way to explain it.

"I also was told my job wasn't a field job," she spoke in a concealed voice. "Another reason I loved it was because after traveling nonstop for the university, I was most excited to sit on my butt and not go anywhere. I was there only to oversee contracts." She tossed a glance over her shoulder, as if she was nervous to be seen. "Why did his guys have you go when it's against his instructions?"

"They didn't even know I was going to Naples today. It was never about the condo." I trapped my bottom lip with my teeth while she gave me a look I had only recently seen in my dreams. I dropped my voice in volume but increased its urgency. "I didn't need to come down here. It was the excuse I needed to get you out of the office so we could talk."

"So, you lied to me." Her gaze narrowed but didn't flinch.

My stomach twisted, signaling my nerves to fire. "I didn't mean to. I mean, not like that. I needed a chance to explain. I knew you'd avoid me in the office, *if* you even came in."

"Explain what to me?" Her *t* was extra sharp and seemed to echo. It wasn't a good idea to have this conversation in public. Then again, she'd never go anywhere alone with me. At least here, she wouldn't make a big scene.

Or maybe she would?

"It hurts." I ran a hand through my hair, taking a moment to hydrate my lips, and decided it was either now or never, and I spilled my heart. "It kills me to see you and think about what I did to you."

"Good. I hope it hurts!" she whispered-shouted back at me but dropped her voice as soon as the bartender looked over. "I hope you're miserable," she hissed. "That's what you deserve!"

"I do deserve it. I was wrong to cut you out without at least explaining everything."

"What is there to explain?" She gestured with both hands, inviting me to talk. "That I thought you had died, or something drastically wrong had happened to you? You didn't even have the decency to explain that you were fine and living your best life with Daddy billionaire. You lied to me about *everything.* You said you wanted to be with me."

"That was never a lie. That was the honest truth. I wanted to be with you, but I wasn't good enough for you."

She curtly nodded, accepting my admittance. "You were right about that last part."

"I'm not that guy anymore." My hands squeezed into fists on the table, as I inhaled a deep breath. "I've already explained this, but I don't know how to make you see that I've changed. If I can't get you to spend time with me, I don't have any way to show you that I'm different."

"And now you are suddenly worthy because you have money? How shallow do you think I am?" She glared at me with her fists clenched. "You were good enough back then. I have no idea who you even are anymore. You literally just brought me to your real estate scam, and you want me to see you've changed?"

"I had no idea about the scam," I hissed over the table. "I'm just as stunned as you are."

"You know what? I'm not even hungry. I'm going to call an Uber." She stood and hustled toward the door. I retrieved some cash from my wallet, dropping it on the table before charging after her. I stormed out the door, and nearly ran into her. She was so close, her soft, wispy scent wafted right to me.

I steeled my knees, firming my stance, determined not to let her leave me. "Elinora." My voice was low, and raspy, catching her attention. I knew it wouldn't pay to blurt out excuses. "I know I messed up. I can't keep making excuses. I thought pretending to be confident and flashing my wealth around would make you like me again. Now I see that was dumb. I know you aren't shallow. I just went too far…That's what I do." My voice cracked but I pushed through it. "You must see that the only thing I want is *you*. You're all I ever wanted. Since I was sixteen." I ran my hand through my hair, pulling it back out of my face, and searched for her eyes, pouring my soul into my words. "I can't change all the ways I've been a jerk, but I'm done pretending I'm fine without you. I need you in my life. I know I can't force you to trust me, and I'm willing to earn it, but please give me a shot."

Her lips parted, before her shaken words spit out with fire, "I've loved you since I was sixteen."

Her angered admission sent a tidal wave of emotions to flood my heart, and I was so over and done with words. I needed to feel her in my arms. I reached out for her hip, and I wrapped my other arm around her waist, pulling her to me as I pressed my lips to hers. I held back, almost as if asking permission, but she kissed me hungrily. Instantly, the magnetism I'd always felt for her budded again in my heart. I was breathless when I pulled away first because I refused to go too far again. I pleaded, "I want you." Her eyes were honest when her guard went down. I was finally getting through to her.

Just when we were making progress, her Uber pulled up at the curb, and the guy signaled toward her with a wave. Her gaze went back and forth between us, and she sputtered out, "I'm so confused right now."

"About what?" I pressed, as she had just kissed me back. That was pretty clear to me what she meant. I wasn't confused about anything. I'd never been clearer about us needing to be together.

"I don't know, but I need to think." She stepped toward the Uber, calling back with her gaze fixed away from me, "I can't do this now."

Twenty-Three

GRAHAM

"That's not what you were wearing when I dropped you off this morning." The following day, I rose to my feet the second Hadley entered my office promptly after nine. "And why are you not at school?" My eyes flashed to my phone, screen up. There wasn't even a text message from her.

"I got sent home to change, but I figured I needed to be honest with you." Her long blonde hair was pulled over her shoulder, and she twirled the end of one strand while avoiding my gaze.

"Yeah, you do." I tried not to stare. Her shorts were so tiny, I swore I could see her underwear hanging out the bottom. "Don't tell me this is the style. You know the rules—the school rules and mine. Neither allows for shorts so tiny." Not wanting my colleagues to overhear, I crossed the room, and shut the door. "Hads, this conversation is exhausting me. You're lucky to have gotten a spot at St. Anne's. Private schools aren't required to put up with defiance. If they get as frustrated as I am, they may permanently suspend you."

"Whatever." She tossed her hair behind her shoulder, as if that was some sort of weapon to win an argument.

"Not whatever." I took a step forward, placing a hand on her shoulder, and squared my gaze with hers. "I want you to succeed in school, have the chances I never had. You'll regret it if you lose this opportunity over something so stupid as shorts." I slipped off my suit jacket, hanging it on her shoulders. As I suspected, it covered more of her rear than her shorts did.

"I'm not wearing your jacket." She lifted her hand to remove it from her shoulders, but I placed my hand on top of hers.

"You're not walking around like that." I didn't flinch when I squeezed her palm. "You can wear those shorts when you're married," I affirmed, stepping back to my desk to grab my phone and keys. "In thirty years."

"*Dad.*"

"I'll give you a ride home to change." I turned back to her, softening my gaze. I'd never imagined I would be the parent who spoke firmly like this. I wanted to be the fun parent. When I looked at her, nearly all grown up, all I wanted to do was protect her as like she was still a wide-eyed four-year-old. "I know you think you're old enough to dress like this, but

I can't allow it. It doesn't show the respect for yourself that you deserve, and it attracts the wrong attention."

"Whatever." Her gaze slid to the ground, as she was clearly avoiding mine.

"Hads..." I spoke even softer. "We've been through too much together to have some stupid shorts cause a huge fight." Opening my arms, I invited her for a hug, and even though she still didn't look at me, she paced forward and allowed me to squeeze her. She was almost as tall as me, clearly having inherited our mom's tall genes. She stood stiff, not hugging me back, but I'd come to terms with what teenage hugs would feel like.

The door flew open, and Elinora halted in the doorway. Her jaw dropped, and she spun on her heel, backing right out. "Wait," I called after her. "It's just Had—" She wasn't listening to me, and I beckoned to Hads. "Follow me. We need to introduce you to everyone in the office before rumors get started."

Twenty-Four

ELINORA

I wasn't stupid. I know what I walked in on—Graham with some blonde, the day *after* he'd practically begged me to be with him. Last night I was ready to quit. I'd planned to max out my credit cards to buy out my contract. I couldn't do this anymore. This morning, I'd had a slight change of heart, wanting to hear him out. My mind had been a ping-pong match all morning. Now I stood firm. Graham was a jerk, and I needed to get away.

He would follow me out the door, and he knew where I lived. It was best to lose him by tricking him, making him believe I'd left the office. That's why I was crouched in the janitor's closet, trying hard to not look at the dead gator I had forgotten I'd stuffed in here earlier this week.

I was used to my dad's projects, but being this close to one in the dark gave me the creeps. I had to hold him upright with one hand, pushing him all the way against the back wall. There still wasn't enough room for us both to be comfortable, and his scales brushed against my leg. Ignoring them as much as I could, I pressed my ear against the door, and listened to make sure Graham had left the office. Just as I suspected, he was looking for me.

Graham: "Mabel, did you see Elinora leave?"

Holding my breath, I silently begged her to cover for me.

Mabel: "I-I did. She ran out that door."

Graham: "I don't understand how she got out of here so fast. I was right behind her."

I pressed my ear closer to the door, as his voice was muffled. The door must not have been latched all the way. Before I could stop myself, I tumbled out, dragging the gator with me.

"Ah!" Mabel and the other female with Graham shrieked, while Graham jumped back a full foot.

"Elinora!" Mabel cried as she jumped on her chair. "You have a gator on you!"

"It's dead!" I called out, before things got out of hand. "It's stuffed, and I'm mostly okay." Rubbing my arm where I'd landed, I sat up and slowly raised my eyes to Graham's, ready to expose him for the cheater he was. My gaze slid to the female, who had high cheekbones and wide eyes the *same color as my mother's ring...*

"You've met Hadley before." Graham nodded in her direction while he walked forward, extending a hand to help me up. "She's here visiting me."

"Ah." Heat rose to my cheeks. Of course I remembered Hadley, but I didn't think for a moment she'd be *this* grown up. "Y-yeah, you are so much older," I stuttered, making sure my jaw wasn't flapping down. "H-how are you?"

"I'm good," she quipped, drawing her attention to Graham. "How do I know her?"

"This is Elinora. You met her when you were little."

Hadley raised her chin in a long, affirming nod. "The dandelion girl."

My insides froze. I fought not to look at Graham, but my heart needed his expression, that magnetism that had always pulled us together, and I could see so clearly in his eyes the vulnerability he felt hearing Hadley say that. He didn't deny it. "Yeah, that's her."

The heat on my cheeks flushed even warmer. "Anybody need a gator?" I diverted the attention away from me as I picked up the taxidermied creature and heaved him back into the closet. "It was a present for my office, before that got hijacked."

"That's not a bad idea." Graham playfully glared at Hadley. "What do you think, Hads? If you keep dressing like this, I'm going to need one. Should we put it on our doorstep?"

"You're so buggin'." She spun on her heel and marched toward the door. "Are you coming, Dad?"

Graham's gaze danced around my face. "I wasn't sure if you were coming in today."

"I wasn't sure if I'd come in today."

"Right." He lowered his voice, but it was pointless because we both knew Mabel had ears like a hawk. "I need to take Hadley back home to change clothes. When I get back, can we talk about last night?"

I stared, blinking at him, wanting to deny we had anything to speak about. "Ah, sure."

"Dad." Hadley's voice sliced through the tension still growing between Graham and me. "I'm going to miss English."

He planted a hesitant foot. "Later, we'll talk." Then he hastened toward Hadley, calling back, "Don't go anywhere until I get back."

Twenty-Five

GRAHAM

Were pink slips even a thing anymore? Those would be too easy. Nowadays, work separation involved more papers than an international peace treaty. I stared at the papers I'd had Human Resources get ready for Elinora.

I realized something after we kissed last night. I didn't want her to be my employee. Desperate for her to hear me out, I had clung to the idea that I could force her to see how I had changed. I had been certain that since I found success, she'd forgive me. I was a fool. None of that mattered to her. It only made her hate me more. I needed to let it go. I wasn't going to force myself on her. That was the wrong way to do this.

Once again, I had gone too far.

I'd been living in the past for too long. I was going to tell her all that. After I thought about it, I realized that even that seemed selfish. A part of me was holding on to her, needing to use any excuse to see her, which wasn't healthy. She didn't want to talk to me, or even see me. She'd made that clear. It was time I finally listened and gave her exactly what she wanted.

A clean break.

Actually, going through even last years' worth of shady business deals at this place, I was ready to let it all go, including my dreams of inheriting Jonathan's billion-dollar company. I had been living in a fantasy land, thinking this dad-son duo was what I needed. Not only was I prepared to let Elinora go today, but I was going to walk out too.

This wasn't me.

The lights in the offices had already started to dim as people locked up to return home. I had texted Elinora I was back in the office and wanted to talk. She'd never replied as she was avoiding me.

I'd finally gotten the hint.

I loosened my tie, inhaling a deep breath, reflecting on all the insane things that had run through my head these last few days. I'd been up all night, thinking about this. I swore my brain formed a callus. I wished I could say I didn't know what had gotten into me, but I did know.

Opening my work bag, I pulled out our notebook. Somewhere over the years, it had become a symbol for this stupid fantasy I had held onto in my head. It was time to let that go as well. The minutes on the clock seemed to stay frozen, and my fingers jittered, needing a fidget of some sort. I grabbed my pen, turned to the first blank page, and started to write an apology, but all I could think of was what a waste of love I was. No matter where I tried to find a home, I was rejected. After scribbling a few lines of apology, I set the book on top of Elinora's stack of papers.

Twenty-Six

My work flats squished my toes as I crept back to my office, trying to go unnoticed. It was easy to do since most people had already left for the day. I'd hung out in the janitor's closet for the last half hour while I waited for Graham to return. I couldn't handle small talk because I was dealing with a serious truth problem, and only one person could help me.

The thing was . . .

Well, I'm not sure what the *thing* was, but I knew my person was Graham. As much as I hated the mistakes he had made, I understood them. He wasn't perfect but he was a great dad, and the only reason he had ghosted me was because he was too hard on himself. He doubted I could love him if things were hard. I couldn't even blame him for that, because that was what he'd learned about love as a child from his mom's abandonment. Now that he was being honest about this stupid cocky façade he'd been wearing, I was ready to be honest too.

I'd always known he was my person.

I couldn't deny it anymore. We had a lot to talk about. Starting with our work situation that was never going to work...and ending with that kiss. My inner monologue rambled as I tried to piece my thoughts together. My heart thumping like a bass drum on my ribs, I slowed right before I got to my office. I pinned on what I liked to refer to as my constipation smile as I walked into my office and found it empty.

Graham had left.

A stack of papers was on my desk. Anger rose, as he was the one who had insisted we talk today. He'd bailed before we could have a conversation and stiffed me with a pile of work! Nothing was more deafening than this silence. I needed to talk this out, but he was clearly a man who couldn't communicate. Was he going to pretend we hadn't kissed?

A snotty snort leaked from my lips as I crossed the office, my eyes landing on a notebook. Not just any notebook but one that melted my insides. I slowed my pace even more as I walked to it and found a bookmark on the last page. My hand trembled when I flipped to that page and read.

I was a dreamer, a waste of love.
Stumbling through life, getting shoved.
You were a giver with a pure heart.

A beautiful gift, my perfect counterpart.
The day I thought forever,
Was every day with you.
But I wasn't worth it.
I needed to become worthy, setting out to find myself.
I found my identity, and it brought great wealth.
The money didn't bring me happiness.
It magnified an emptiness.
Finding myself only brought memories of you.
I'm sorry.
I had HR draw up your severance papers. You're free.

This was the first time I'd ever read anything in this book that made me stain the page with tears. Frustration. Fear. Regret. Years of unrequited love flashed through my mind. Dropping the notebook, I glanced over my papers. Everything was effective immediately. I didn't have to buy out my contract. He'd even included severance pay, but I couldn't accept any of this. I needed to talk this out. I wasn't going to let him ghost me, *again.*

I yanked my phone out of my pocket and constructed a text as I strode back down the hall, ready to go after him. I had learned the last time that he didn't reply to texts when he was ghosting me, and I wasn't going to let that happen again.

Wham!

I bounced right off his chest where he stood blocking the door. He hadn't gotten away from me just yet. With a whoosh of a step back, I steeled my gaze with his. "You're not going to get away with this again!"

His neutral expression crumbled as his eyes danced over my face. "What's wrong?"

"What's wrong?" I dropped an unladylike snort. To be fair, all snorts were considered unladylike. We'll classify this noise more like a hack. "We were going to talk about things, but you left. *Again.*"

"No." His baritone voice held firm. "I could never ghost you again, but I gave you what you wanted, your separation from Platinum Real Estate. I don't expect you to expose yourself to the illegal real estate ring."

"What are you really doing?" My heart thumped in pain like someone had taken a chisel to it.

His brows angled up, but his expression was firm. "I'm getting ready to bring the police in and let them know what's going on. I'll be putting in my notice as well."

"No, Graham. Not what you are doing with work. We kissed." There was that hack again, and yes, I was the one making that most unflattering noise. "I thought you wanted to talk about us."

"About that." He blew out a breath as he sliced his hand through his hair, leaving a wispy strand of hair to dangle by his cheek. "I'm not sorry about that. That needed to happen for me to see how crazy I was being, and maybe it's the closure I needed."

"Closure!" I dropped another unflattering noise, this one was more like a hiccup. My words were shorting out. "That kiss..." The heat in my face fired again as I recalled how his lips had melted on mine. I didn't have any doubt he had genuine feelings for me, but it was impossible to explain all of this. I finally understood everything. "The last thing I want is closure."

His head took a curious angle, a hint of a sideways glance. The reflections in his eyes sparkled as he slowly connected the dots. "You don't need closure?"

"I don't." I flashed the notebook I was still holding back at him. "I understand everything now. I'm ready to forgive you." With a boldness I'd never had before, I took a step forward and raised my chin. "I think we need to do that kiss again."

He lowered his mouth, our lips so geographically close that I could feel the warmth from his breath. "Isn't awkward kissing how we got into this whole mess in the first place?"

I snaked an arm around his neck as goosebumps prickled my arm. "But if it got us into this mess, I'm certain it's the remedy to get us out."

"Is that how it works?" He touched my chin, tipping it up until our lips crashed together, and all my anxieties melted away. This wasn't our first kiss. It wasn't even our best kiss, but it was a moment that brought us together, finally over our hurdles. When it was over, we linked hands and strolled out of that office together.

"Where do we go now?" I asked, as we closed our office door together, knowing we'd never step foot in there again.

"Anywhere but here." He slowed as we passed into the parking lot. "Where do you want to go?"

"I heard Vermont is nice." I gently elbowed him in the rib, teasing a flashback to our youth.

"Yeah, I know a bookstore that needs a manager. It's in a simple little town, nothing fancy. Actually, quite boring."

"Sounds perfect."

Twenty-Seven

GRAHAM

One month later

I tugged at my collar, trying to get some air as sweat pooled on the back of my neck. I had just packed a U-Haul and was ready to leave this town in my rearview mirror for good. There was one thing I needed to do. I'd been dreading it. I shuffled my feet on Elinora's parents' front step. Raising my fist, ready to knock on the front door, I froze.

I couldn't do it.

This would be so much easier with Elinora here.

I swiped my hand through my hair and replanted my fist on the front of the door. My gut said I needed to be a man about this. I sucked in a deep breath and rapped on the door. Maybe I should have called ahead just to give fair warning? Sometimes catching people off-guard could make things worse than they really were. I wasn't even sure what Elinora had exactly said to her parents about me over the years, the bad or the good. The door pulled open, and I prayed for Elinora's mom.

Just another unanswered prayer.

I got Ron standing in his bathrobe and plaid house slippers. He had aged a considerable amount, now having more hair in his ears than on the top of his head. He also appeared to have shrunk since the last time I had seen him. My eyes narrowed as I tried not to stare, but he had changed so much. He wasn't at all the tall, slender, threatening man I had known in my youth. This guy was chubby, a full spare tire around his middle, and old. "I'm sorry if I've caught you at a bad time." I started to turn, the quibbles in my gut getting more violent with each second. I wasn't cut out for this.

"Graham." Ron took a step out on the porch, shutting the door behind him. "You don't need to leave."

"You remember who I am?" I steeled my feet into position, staying a measure away from him in case I needed a running start.

"I've been waiting for you to stop by sometime. Elinora's been talking about you an awful lot again."

"Er, um, I hope it's all good." I tucked my hands behind my back, wringing them together, wishing so hard Ron didn't know everything wrong I'd ever done.

He blinked, with no reassurance that anything he'd heard was good, and sweat poured off of my lower back at an alarming rate. I wanted to bolt, but I came here for a purpose. I couldn't leave without at least trying. "Look," I breathed out. "I know what you think of me, but you knew me many years ago. I was a kid who came from a very broken home. I'm not that guy anymore. I'm not the kid who threw a fit because he couldn't play football. I, ah…" I shoved my hands in my pockets, and suddenly, Hadley's face flashed before my eyes. I blinked, but she was all I saw.

Ron obviously still stood there with one hand propped against the deck support beam, glaring at me through narrowed eyes, as if he was waiting for me to choke.

Everything clicked, and I stuttered out, "I-I have a daughter. She's fourteen, going on thirty, and she's a little piece of heaven I never deserved. I fight every day not to break her. I think she's too perfect for this screwed-up world, and that nobody will treat her as well as I do. While I love her with every fiber of my being, she's also the single person who knows how to pluck every last nerve I have. I get it…" My voice trailed off, because although Hadley was still too young to date—*she'd better not even be thinking about it*—I would go to jail for her if I could ensure she'd be safe forever. I certainly wouldn't be above scaring off any random scum who showed up on my doorstep, trying to spend time with her.

Ron wasn't a psycho. Okay, maybe he'd gone a little too far with the taxidermy pheasants on the deck, and I would never look at a squirrel the same way again, but he had clearly panicked, not prepared to see his daughter grow up. As I stood staring at the bags under Ron's eyes and the almost bare scalp that used to house a whole head of hair, I understood him. I actually appreciated him. He'd protected Elinora from me when I could have really messed her up. She had been so innocent and had no clue about the world where I'd grown up. He'd also probably protected her from other losers. With Ron's protection and the grace of God, she was still the soft-hearted person who'd loved me through all my stages. Oddly, I had Ron to partially thank for that. "I, ah, just want to say thank you for raising Elinora the way you did. There are some days I think I could use a stuffed bear or two to help with my daughter. I...ah, understand now."

His lips smashed together, and for a moment I thought he was going to crack a smile. Maybe. Something was clearly going on, and he was fighting it. "I hate this," he finally grumbled, but he stuck out his hand, offering a handshake.

"I know." I took his hand, gripping it firmly as I prepared for an old-fashioned squeezing match. This was Ron, after all, and he wasn't going to give up fighting for his baby girl so easily.

"You're sticking around this time, aren't you?" He took his hand back, shoving it in his pocket, his expression still unchanged.

"I'd like to." I lifted one corner of my lips into a slight grin. "If you don't have the cops drag me off again."

"Oh." He blew out a deep breath, wagging his head back and forth. "I'd sure like to." He chuckled, his lips finally cracking into a close approximation of a smile. "Thought about it, but I think I'm going to have to let go this time. Some things are just too strong to fight."

"I love her." Now it was my turn to smash my lips together—I knew exactly what he was talking about. I'd tried to ignore the magnetism I'd felt for Elinora from the first day, but twenty years later, we were still finding our way back to each other, and though neither of us was perfect, we were ready to give this forever thing a go. I smiled at Ron, and I knew we'd never be friends. We'd never be buds who called each other up before the big game and placed bets, but I could see in his expression that he was wearing a respect for me he'd never had before. I could live with that.

Actually, I was excited to live with that.

It meant I could move forward with Elinora.

Twenty-Eight

Elinora

Six Months Later

I hurried down the courthouse steps and looked up to find the most beautiful eyes staring back at me. With my backpack slung over one shoulder, I linked my arm in his, and we strolled home from my first day at my new job. I had snagged a very part-time contract job with no benefits working with the city attorney. Graham had surprised me by meeting me at work, and even though it was only across the street, my heart melted when I realized how lucky I was. I got to walk home with Graham every day. Mapleton, Vermont was a dream town, with quaint brick sidewalks, and all the residents seemed to walk around with secret-holding smiles on their faces. We'd quickly fallen into our lives here, not looking back for a moment.

"Did you see Jonathan's latest indictment on the news?" I spoke in a hushed voice, even though the streets were mostly bare. "And his wife just got up and left him. I don't blame her. I wouldn't want to get dragged into his scams."

"I briefly heard before I turned it off." He shrugged his shoulders dismissively. "I can't really stomach that stuff."

"I'm sorry to bring it up."

"It's okay. I know it's necessary to acknowledge, but I'm ready to go home, and spend the evening relaxing. What do you want to do?"

"Honestly, I'm happy to be in our little apartment with you and Hadley."

"I'm happy you are here with us, too." He promptly tucked his phone away and grabbed my hand. As he linked his fingers to mine, he twisted the ring on my left hand. It was simple, like me. A white gold band. I had decided to forgo a traditional diamond, instead, opting for a blue sapphire, colored like the eyes of the man I love.

We waited six months to marry, even though we would have both eloped the very next day after we left our office. We knew Hadley needed some time to adjust. All my trepidation about being a stepmom had easily vanished when Hadley fast became part of my whole world because our relationship was natural and the three of us grew together as a little family.

Graham and I had a simple wedding and an outdoor reception with the Vermont spring foliage and homemade dandelion strings as our only décor. My dad had even given us his blessing to get married, as he'd said he "sort of always knew." It was everything I'd never known I wanted, and it filled my heart with everything I'd needed.

Our lives were simple here in this small town.

Our small family.

I'd never been happier. We arrived in front of our apartment, but before we opened the door, we stopped, sharing one of our secret looks, and I leaned in for a kiss. It wasn't awkward anymore. We'd gotten quite good at kissing each other.

Dear Reader, Thank you for reading Elinora and Graham's sweet story. When I decided to give the series a glowup with new covers, I added an extended bonus scene to give us a chance to catch up with this fun couple a year later. Keep turning the pages to find out what they are up to!

Twenty-Nine

A Year Later

Elinora

When I told my best friend, Bre, that Graham, Hadley, and I are "totally making it work" in Graham's old one-bedroom apartment, she laughed and said, "That sounds so cute and cozy for about five minutes."

Okay, I admit, she wasn't entirely wrong.

At first, it really was *so* cute.

And *so* cozy.

Hadley got her old bedroom back. She wasn't exactly ecstatic about downgrading her life so much by returning to this apartment, but it makes sense for her to get the bedroom. Teenagers need privacy, and a solid wood door to slam whenever her hormonal moods take over.

With her in the only room, Graham and I had one option: the couch.

Or, more specifically, the pull-out couch with a mattress thin enough to make my entire body scream in protest after only two very long, sleepless nights.

But that first night?

It had been a little romantic bliss.

We giggled and curled under our shared blanket with the flickering glow of the streetlight outside leaking through the blinds. Graham, my sweet new husband, pressed up behind me, his breath tickling the back of my neck. "You know," he murmured, "this is everything I have always dreamed of."

"Me too," I whispered back, stifling a laugh so we wouldn't wake Hadley. Being together as husband and wife was my happy ever after. I closed my eyes and drifted off to the happiest sleep, as Graham kissed my shoulder and rolled over.

I totally bought into this living situation.

Corny, yes.

But I was all heart eyes as we tangled together. At some point, I eventually drifted off to sleep with my cheek pressed to his chest like Graham was my life preserver. When I woke up, I breathed a sigh of relief that he was still here, exactly how he was when I fell asleep.

Life was perfect.

Thirty

GRAHAM

The honeymoon phase of the couch didn't last long.

We are in week three, and the apartment has started to feel like it's shrinking. It was small when I lived here before. I remind myself that Hadley was three back then and took up a lot less space. Now, we have added a third person, and it feels like the walls are closing in.

Man, I love them both more than anything.

But love didn't magically make a one-bedroom apartment any bigger, and it doesn't make living with two unique female personalities any easier.

The pull-out couch has developed a permanent sag in the middle. Every night Elinora and I roll toward each other whether we feel like snuggling or not. At first it was funny and actually the perfect excuse to pull her closer and bury my face in her hair. But after a ten-hour day at the bookshop, my back cries for mercy and space to stretch out.

Not to mention there's a bit of an airflow issue. Like there's too many scents in too small of a space. Left over aromas waft from the kitchen and mingle with the bathroom scents that drift in from the other side of the room. I don't exactly complain, as I'm so incredibly blessed by this life and for everything Elinora gave up to move to Mapleton.

She never complains, so of course I can't.

But I accidentally start staying late at the bookshop.

Not to avoid them!

I always enjoy spending time with them but to prevent us all from suffocating.

The first night, I tell myself the store tile floor needs a good mopping. I clean for an extra hour, and then I lie down on the worn leather couch in my office. I stretch my legs out and have room to lie flat on my back, and a random thought pops in my head:

Just tonight, I could sleep here.

I'm too tired to move. Even though it's just another couch, it's all to myself, which means I will likely get more sleep here than upstairs. Before I talk myself out of it, I text Elinora:

Hey, I stretched out on the couch in my office, and now I'm too sore to move. I'm just going to rest down here for a while.

Elinora doesn't complain when I text her. In fact, she seems a little eager to have a whole couch to herself.

Her: Okay...sounds good.

Then "just tonight" turns into two nights.

It's not that I don't want to be with her.

I want nothing more than to snuggle for hours.

Every time I crawl into that sagging couch-bed, I suffocate. There is no space for me, no air to breathe, and it's like relaxing on concrete. I feel like I'm being crushed.

And that terrifies me.

After everything Elinora and I have been through, the last thing I want is for her to think I need space from her. So, after the second night of sleeping downstairs, I return to our bed. Sweat actually slaps on my lower back as I struggle with the very thought of sleeping on this sorry excuse for a mattress, but Elinora needs me. So, I kiss her goodnight and hug her like I mean it—which I do. Then, when she falls asleep, I find myself tossing, turning, and spitting out random strings of her hair that I somehow almost swallow. After an hour, I give up and do the unthinkable.

I leave her.

Clearly, it's a noble decision.

The most unselfish thing.

I'm simply giving her the space so she can sleep well.

But deep down, I know the truth: I'm avoiding the conversation.

Because admitting I hate our living situation feels like I'm criticizing her. And I'd rather break my back on the bookstore couch than risk making her feel like she isn't enough.

Thirty-One

ELINORA

The first night Graham didn't come back upstairs, I thought it was funny and sort of nice to have the bed to myself.

But then it happened again.

And then he vowed it wouldn't happen again.

At which point, he started sneaking around after he thought I was sleeping.

I hate it.

I hate whenever I try to sleep, I inhale whatever we had for dinner still left in the air. I hate the only privacy I get with my husband is the five minutes it takes us to brush our teeth at the same sink in the tiny bathroom. I hate there is clutter everywhere because we don't have enough storage. But most of all, I hate Graham's choosing a leather couch downstairs over me.

Sure, he sneaks back up in the morning. I pretend to be sleeping, so he won't feel bad. He slips back into bed next to me. At which point, I pretend to wake up and plant a pleased-to-see-you smile on my face as I kiss him good morning.

"Morning," he says.

I arch a brow. "Morning? That's what I get?"

"What do you mean?"

"You've been sleeping downstairs." My voice cracks. "Do you really think I wouldn't notice?"

He rubs a hand over his jaw. "I didn't want to wake you."

"Or you didn't want to sleep next to me."

"That's not—" He stops himself. His eyes are tired. "I love you," he says, low and fierce. "This isn't about that. It's us having the space to rest."

I blink at the weariness he's not hiding anymore. And for once, instead of pretending everything's fine, I say the words that have been bubbling in my chest since the day we moved in. "Graham, I know this place saves us money, and it's sentimental to you and all, but we need a house."

He lets out a startled laugh, like I'd announced we should buy a cruise ship. "A house?"

"Yes, a house." I gesture toward the kitchen that's a couple of steps away. "It doesn't have to be anything fancy or even expensive, but we can't live life like this. We need space during the day, so at night you aren't avoiding me. I need you next to me, not sneaking off to a couch downstairs."

His expression is neutral, as he's not giving me any clues to how upset he really is about this. "You're serious."

"As serious as I've ever been."

He blinks at me like I've said the most unreasonable thing. Then the corners of his mouth tip up. "All right," he says. "If that's what you need, let's buy a house."

I let out a deep breath, and my chest unknots, feeling so much better already.

Thirty-Two

GRAHAM

Why is it in the movies house hunting looks adorable?

A matching-sweater-wearing couple walks into a sunny kitchen, points at the breakfast nook, and laughs about how perfect it will be for Saturday brunch with the in-laws. That's all it takes, and they sign on the dotted line.

In reality, most houses have a random smell I can't stomach and a price tag that makes me sweat. Even after working in real estate all those years, it's not any easier because our budget is tiny.

The first house we look at... let's just call it *something special.*

The front door sticks before swinging open with a groan that sounds like the opening scene to every single *Nightmare on Elm Street* movie. I glance back at Elinora, who raises her eyebrows like, "After you, my brave husband, who thought this was a good idea."

We pass through the door and enter the kitchen. I take one tiny breath, almost gag, and whisper to her, "If *someone died in here* had a signature fragrance, it would be this."

She laughs, as she motions toward the cabinets that have doors hanging at odd angles. "Solid craftsmanship," she says with an air of sarcasm. "I'm sure that's what the listing meant by the vintage charm."

"Oh, totally." I step back. "I can already see you opening that and ending up in urgent care."

She grins. "Okay, I feel like I've seen enough. There's no way we could afford what it would cost to renovate this kitchen, and honestly, I don't even want this house."

"Right," I say, already heading out the door we just came in. "Let's leave before the realtor spots us and traps us with his sale's speech..."

***

The second open house has promise, judging from its curb appeal, but I'm not feeling optimistic when we stand on the stoop together. Elinora presses her lips together and opens the door as the real estate agent is inside the door waiting. She whispers, "Yikes, we just got spotted. Now we can't make a clean escape this time."

I hold back my chuckle as I flash a wave to the woman standing inside, and Elinora and I step over the threshold single file into a living room. The first thing I notice is the paint needs refreshing, but that's not structural. I can handle a few cosmetic things, and paint isn't all that expensive. I walk over the wood floor that oddly still has some sheen to it, and it doesn't creak when I walk. *Hmm, must be made well.*

We're quiet as we pass into the kitchen that is clean and modest, but all the cabinets hang straight. When we tour the three bedrooms, which all have enough natural lighting we didn't need to flip on the light switch, I start to feel like this might be a home we can live in.

Elinora feels it too.

I swear her entire body changes as soon as she sees the second bathroom. Her eyes soften, she finally looks like she can breathe because there's no detectible odor, other than a light lemon-scented cleaner.

"This one," she whispers as she pops her head out of the master bathroom and grabs my elbow when the realtor isn't looking.

My heart squeezes.

Because yes, it's perfect, with the white-picket fence and matching shutters. It has a nice big backyard that we could use for so many things and ample room for the three of us.

The caveat?

It's so insanely out of our price range, I nearly choke. "Babe, you saw the price on this one, right?"

"I did, but I can apply to a full-time job at one of the law offices in town. Something has to turn up." She looks so hopeful as she bats her lashes at me. The way the late light filters in through the large living room window shadows her face so perfectly. *This is a home for a family, and it's exactly what we need. She deserves this*

However, as much as I agree with her this house is perfect, I spike a hand through my hair and tighten my jaw. I don't have a clue how we can afford this. I hate to put all the financial stress on her to work more. I really want to be a provider. The bookstore is barely above breaking even, and that's why the free apartment upstairs makes so much sense. Yet, as much sense as it makes, it doesn't actually work.

I can't tell her no. I smile at her and whisper, so the real estate agent doesn't hear, "Yeah, it's perfect. We just need to go over our budget, but everything should work out."

Thirty-Three

ELINORA

Back at the apartment, that perfect house haunts me. Every time I bump or pull out the couch bed, or trip over the shoes piled by the door, I see *that* living room with the wide-open floor plan and that spacious coat closet by the front door.

But most of all, I feel the way it felt like home before we even said a word.

Then reality hits me as soon as I try to turn on the tiny apartment stove. Oh, the burners have other ideas than dinner. The front left one never worked for me, but today the back right sparks once and then goes dark. Startling me, I jump back to catch my breath. *It's not supposed to do that!*

I'd like to order a pizza, as I don't even feel safe in this kitchen, but my gaze floats to the pack of chicken I've laid out on the counter. I can't waste it, and dinner is not going to cook itself. As much as I hate this stove, I won't be eating raw chicken anytime soon. Sighing, I stand back as far as I can and reach out with a straight elbow, ready to test the third burner. Graham bursts through the front door.

"Don't tell me." He strides toward me. "Something is wrong with the stove."

My jaw drops from his mind reading abilities. "How'd you know?"

He raises a brow. "Well, the downstairs lights kept flickering, so I knew you were doing something, and your facial expression tells me all I need to know."

An easy laugh slips out of my lips. I love how, even in the middle of this mess, he can still make me laugh.

Yanking his phone out of his pocket, he flashes it at me for a second before saying, "I don't think it's safe. Just step away until I have time to look at it. I'll order pizza."

My stomach loves that idea. At least dinner is taken care of now. I swipe the chicken off the counter and return it to the fridge, as my shoulders drop in relief.

That solves my problem tonight.

But what about the next night?

And the one after that.

This stove is a wreck.

I don't know if it's worth replacing it. My mind floats back to that kitchen we saw earlier. It had a nice big island in the middle and updated stainless-steel appliances that shine. I bet I'd actually love cooking in that kitchen...

Thirty-Four

GRAHAM

I stay in bed all night, but zero sleep comes to me. I can tell Elinora is worried about something because she is also up tossing and turning. I don't want to get caught sneaking down to the couch. Surprisingly, she's the one who sneaks out of bed early. When she doesn't return, I suspect she's gone down to the couch. Chuckling, I quickly throw a shirt on and freeze when I notice the front door is still bolted shut from the night.

She's somewhere in this apartment.

My eyes slam to the bathroom where, sure enough, light filters in from the crack. Crossing the apartment in a few long strides, I slip my head in the door uninvited. Elinora is pacing the two-foot space. Her bare feet slap against dull linoleum in the pattern that warns if I say one wrong word, I'm a dead man.

The trouble is, I don't know what I did wrong.

I stayed in bed all night long, and I have the kink in my neck to prove it!

My gaze flows around the room for a leaking pipe or something I need to fix, but then my jaw drops when I see what's on the tiny counter.

Three pregnancy tests lined up like soldiers, all ready to do battle.

All of them have the same result.

Two pink lines.

"Are you serious?" My jaw is still hanging down while every nerve in my body buzzes alive, like I've been handed the best news of my life. I don't wait to be acknowledged, I push the door open and barge in.

She's unable to meet my direct gaze as she seems a tad wobbly and about ready to faint. "This can't be happening." She forgoes a hello and presses both hands to her face. "We can't afford this. We can't—oh man—we just found the house. We don't even know how we can pay for that, and now this!"

It's funny how I imagined this moment before. In all my daydreams, I panic. But this morning, I'm oddly calm as I step forward and gently pry her hands away so I can see her eyes. They are wide and beautiful, even when she's crashing out. "Elinora," I say softly, "don't you see? This is perfect timing."

"Perfect?" She lets out a sharp laugh. "You call this *perfect*? We're crammed in a one-bedroom with a stove that only knows how to shoot off fireworks. There is absolutely nowhere we could even put a crib in here, and the only house we like, we can't afford. We're doomed."

Part of me wants to scoop her into my arms and twirl her around, but she honestly looks as if she's about to throw up. My heart is crawling in my throat and begging me to look at those tests. I pick one up and marvel at it. "Do you know what this means?"

The look of fear she gives me tells me not to pause long enough for her to reply. Instead, I place my hands on her hips and draw her closer to me. "It means that our little family just got bigger. That not only are we buying a house, but we're filling it up. It's the best news ever."

She doesn't say anything while her chin quivers. For a moment, I think she might cry. Instead, she exhales, and says, "Okay, we can do this."

"Yes, we can." I pull her closer to me until her cheek is against my chest, and I rest my chin on the top of her head in my favorite way to hold her.

She lifts her face enough to level her gaze with mine. "So, you're happy about this?"

"I've never been happier." There, in our too-small bathroom, surrounded by clutter and three positive pregnancy tests, I laugh.

Somehow, this is exactly the life I dreamed of. I don't know how we'll afford that house, but I don't know how I did anything I did that was a success. Sometimes things work out, and I don't have a doubt in my mind this is one of those things. The baby is the deciding thing I need to know we need that house.

Suddenly, I can't stop smiling.

My life is a little messier than I would have dreamed up, but I couldn't be happier.

It's my happy ever after.

ALSO BY J.P. STERLING

Bosses and Billionaires Series (All Standalones)
Maid for my Billionaire Boss
Upcycling My Rig-Pig Boss
Marooned with My Celebrity Boss
Kissed by My Billionaire Boss
A Heart that Dances Series
Dancing on Broken Ankles
The Stars We See
A Heart that Dances
A Heart that Loves
Water and Stone Duet
Ruby in the Water
Lily in the Stone
Christmas Shenanigans (All Standalones)
Mingle All the Way
'Tis the Season to get Married.

The Coffee Loft Series (All Standalones)

Pardon My French Press

No More Mr. Chai Guy

About J.P. Sterling

I write wholesome stories and love all things slapstick humor and heart strings.

Aside from writing, I'm also a wife and homeschooling mom, a holistic nutritionist, a jewelry designer, a professional archivist, former college instructor and lover of all things dark chocolate.

Author Clean Code: I like to make my stories about the story and not about a bunch of profanity, mature content, or graphic violence that are only there to shock you. I write my stories to be family friendly.

Guess what amazing thing just happened?

I just launched my own private reading group on Facebook.

Want to be part of my inner circle of readers?

Hop in the group here: https://www.facebook.com/groups/1500850764081965

For free audio books please visit:

https://www.youtube.com/c/JpSterling

Find me on Instagram:

https://www.instagram.com/authorjpsterling/

Sign up to my free monthly newsletter to get the first look at my new books, free book offers and random updates:

https://landing.mailerlite.com/webforms/landing/q9c0v3